I0831407

WBT
PUBLISHING

The Box in the Attic

The Box in the Attic

Tale of the Red Book

by

Paul Alan Richardson

WB Tree Publishing

USA

contact@wbtreepublishing.com

www.paulalanrichardson.com

ISBN (print hardcover): 979-8-9999550-0-5

ISBN (print paperback): 979-8-9999550-1-2

ISBN (ebook): 979-8-9999550-2-9

Published by WB Tree Publishing, LLC

USA

www.wbtreepublishing.com

First edition - November 2025

For

Dreamers,

Friends, and

Heroes

The 1st Tale

- 1 - In the Attic -

My name was written in green marker on a piece of tape across the box in the attic.

Cardboard corners crumbled when I lifted the lid.

The Red Book was inside. I felt 7 years old again.

It'd been decades since I last saw the smooth leather cover and gold rimmed pages. Now the Red Book was mine. I could finally read it. Inside the box I found other objects that rekindled old magic—a piece of string, a quarter, and a mysterious manilla envelope with the words "Only Open After Finishing the Red Book."

Like a blanket pulled over my shoulders, the box brought sudden comfort. Maybe it was the dust fairies drifting in the old attic, or the rain pitter pattering the tin roof, or perhaps the Saturday morning lamplight sparkled something mystical. Whatever the reason, I fell back into the lost days of childhood with hours of free time to drift into a fantasy tale.

I'd only seen the Red Book once before and never opened it. Grandpa convinced me the book was alive, the secret hiding spot of everything astonishing and beautiful in our world.

I found the box as I went through the old man's house, getting it ready to put on the market. As Grandpa said on our last call, "Sell it to whoever needs it most." The funeral was yesterday.

A man of many names—Robert Cattrall, Captain Cattrall, CC, Bob the Cat—Grandpa lived an overflowing life full of adventure, laughter, bear hugs, and pondering the universe's biggest questions.

He could be a bookworm, military man, jolly elf, or boisterous showman. He might have been Leonardo Da Vinci in a past life.

The Red Book was his magical doing. Grandpa read it to me only once. On the day before my golden birthday—I turned 7 on the 7th of June.

School had let out for the summer, but I was stuck in the house. A fever, my mother said, though I felt fine.

I didn't mind. Because Grandpa came to babysit. The old man knew my favorite things—riddles, games, books, adventures, puzzles, and mysteries.

He brought the Red Book that day and said it told the history of *The Land Between the Seas.* It wasn't a regular book of stories you heard from beginning to end. It was a quest. The Red Book talked back to you. It asked questions.

"It's far too dangerous for a 7 year old to hear," Grandpa said with stone seriousness. "When traveling through the Red Book, if we go down one wrong trail, give one wrong answer, then an entire world is destroyed forever."

Sitting on a crate next to the attic window, I stared at the shimmering cover and fell back into the deep Red...

- 1 - In the Living Room –

"What's that red book?" the boy in blue slippers asked from the couch under a fuzzy green blanket. Raindrops rumbled the roof.

A greying eyebrow rose, "That's one of the biggest secrets in the universe."

Grandpa sat in his chair, pulled out the book, and ran a caring hand across the cover. "This is the Red Book. The one and only copy. It preserves the tales of *The Land Between the Seas*, as told in 15 not too long tales."

Blessed with cat curiosity, the boy propped an elbow on a pillow, peered at the book, and asked, "Where is the *The Land Between the Seas*? In the United States?"

"Oh no, it's in another dimension. The Land is the place where Magic itself is born and protected. Anything remarkable, utterly unbelievable, miraculous, and awe-inspiring is created there and transferred here."

The boy's toes wiggled in his slippers. Now he was interested. "Where did you get the Red Book?"

"I received the story from my grandfather, who heard it from his grandmother, who was told by a best friend's uncle. Before that, sometime after the last Ice Age, the line is lost."

Especially clever, his teacher called this particular boy "almost 7 going on 30." He was skeptical of the idea that all the wonder in the world was hidden in a book. But then the boy remembered that the old man twirled quarters and spun cards, like a real magician. They'd once gone to a magic show where men appeared from nowhere, people read one another's minds, and a lady was sawed in half, then combined again.

"Can I read it?" the child asked, staring at the Red Book.

"Absolutely not!" a wrinkled hand wiped his brow as if suddenly sweating. "This book is a Secret. I shouldn't even have brought it here. Unless you know the right order to read the stories, then you risk destroying all it protects, including everything that's wondrous, magical, astonishing, and beautiful on Planet Earth. No no, silly boy, you are far too young for the Red Book. It would be irresponsible of me to even," he stopped talking to the boy and started talking to himself. "Well, I guess, just the one, maybe, as a test, today is his only chance, but is he ready..."

"Since tomorrow is your 7th birthday, the 7th of June, your golden day, I will read you the gateway story into the book. But first the rules..."

"Number One: I cannot answer any questions during a story. It's a magical quest and the Book decides what you hear. I must read every story exactly as written. Number Two: Every tale ends in a question or riddle. It must be answered correctly to lead you to the next story in the proper order. Number Three: If you hear even a single tale after the gateway, then you are obligated to finish the quest or destroy the world trying."

The caretaker stood in front of the boy in the blue slippers, under the green blanket on the long couch, as the rainy day *pitter patter* played through the bay windows. He flipped to a page somewhere in the middle of the Red Book, "Ah, yes, here's the entry tale, *The Origin of the Land Between the Seas...*"

- 1 - *The Origin of The Land Between the Seas*

Once Upon a Time, Long Before Memories, a Nothing twisted into Something. The Something became Everything.

The Everything gave itself a Name. That Name was a Shape. The Shape was also a Sound. Most importantly, the Sound was a Meaning. From that Meaning, the space grew like a garden into a great Land.

A Shape that was a Sound and a Meaning became *The Land Between the Seas.*

The Land rose, fell, shifted, and filled into pools. It exploded into leaves, vines, flowers, mountains, valleys, crevices, fields, and forests with trunks of endless color. Moving creatures sprouted from the garden leaves—some slithering, some sitting, some galloping across the wind. Creations like humans made fires in hidden caves.

Giants of enormous green with solid patched shells called Turtles roamed the mountains. Snakes of all sizes shifted like strings, swirled and danced across the grasses.

Memories developed, and stories were told about who they all were and how they came to be. The earliest creatures knew that the magic that turned Nothing into Something must be preserved. As long as the Name of the Land was remembered this magic would always exist.

Pay close attention, Dear Listener, for if you pass the gateway and accept the Red Book responsibility, then your mission is to find the Shape, Sound, and Meaning of its True Name.

After endless eons, as the oldest stories were replaced by the new, the three parts of this Name were forgotten.

Eventually only two creatures remembered—The Most Beautiful Turtle in all the Land and the Most Astonishing Snake. The Snake could twist into the Shape of the Land, and the Turtle stored the secret of the three under its impenetrable shell. As if sharing a mind, the pair fell in love at first sight and sound.

The two Protectors of the Magic lived together in perfect harmony until one terrible day. Three miserable brothers grew jealous of the wisdom, serenity, and fame of the Turtle and Snake. The brothers discovered the one great weakness of the Protectors—the creatures were incredibly kind.

With a band of thieving others, the miserable brothers tricked the great Protectors of the Magic. They convinced the Beautiful Turtle to go to the bottom of the deepest waters, claiming someone needed help. Then they asked the Astonishing Snake to go to the top of the furthest mountain.

The Soulmates became hopelessly lost from one another. After wandering in loneliness, they disappeared from sight and memory. But a few whisper that the Astonishing Snake and Beautiful Turtle still appear here and there, sharing secrets of the way to the Shape that is a Sound that is a Meaning—the True Name of the *The Land Between the Seas.*

- 1 - In the Living Room -

Grandpa paused, exhaled, stood up, and then finished the entry tale of the Red Book, "Now a question for you, Listener at the Gate. Answer correctly and you get the chance to continue. ***What are the three parts of the True Name that you must find to preserve all the magic there is?***"

The old man continued, "Before you answer, please know two things: This is an opening question to the quest. If you are wrong the gate will lock shut, never budge, and I can't read you a single other story from this book. If you are right, you will be asked if you would like to go on the adventure. But before even considering that, what's your answer? *What are the three parts of the True Name that you must find to preserve all the magic there is?*"

The boy with a near perfect memory belted, "The Shape, Sound, and Meaning."

"Correct, wise little one." Grandpa smiled. "But now comes the hard part."

The 2nd Tale

- 2 - In the Attic -

I prefer reading to listening. But I could always sit and enjoy a story told by Grandpa, the old showman, Captain Cattrall.

Reading came easy, and I learned at a young age. They said it's because my memory was like an ocean, whatever that meant. But I think it's from reading so many of Grandpa's mailed letters. He was prolific at the post office for his stacks of correspondence.

I received so many messages that I memorized his handwriting and could copy it. He started scribbling in different styles with strange pens, he jokingly said, "to protect his identity." Then I remember him saying, "As long as you understand the meaning of the words, then how you shape each letter makes no difference."

He enjoyed little old man quips like that, but I was often too young to understand them. Grandpa once said that he figured out the Meaning of Life in the shower. He wrote it down on the steamy glass door, but it faded before he finished washing off his shampoo. "Now my life's purpose is remembering the shower answer," he said.

He lived for the long joke and endless game. Like finally leaving me the Red Book, only decades later.

The one day he read it to me, I wondered if it was written in another language. I could never be sure, because I never saw inside. Not even a single letter. Grandpa would carefully open to just the right page, sometimes checking an index. I only saw the flashes of gold edges circling the red.

As a budding 7 year old in blue slippers, I believed I held the entire world on my shoulders when Grandpa asked with a sigh, "What decision would you like to make next?"

- 2 - In the Living Room -

Grandpa explained, "Since you answered the question correctly, the gate has unlocked for you. But, you do not have to enter and hear the next tale."

The storyteller was still standing in front of the boy on the couch. He ran a tanned hand through his greying hair, and paced one length of the living room.

"The choice is yours alone. If I close the book, you cannot ever hear another story in it. If I read the next tale, you must continue until you either answer a riddle incorrectly or take a wrong path when a choice is given to you. Do you understand?"

The boy nodded and shivered. A decision must be made.

Grandpa exhaled, wiped a brow with a handkerchief, and said with hands behind his back, "Before you choose, I must issue the warning: If you fail in this mission, the stakes are nothing less than the destruction of an entire world. *The Land Between the Seas* will no longer exist in that invisible place beyond our sight."

He wiped his forehead again and nearly wept as he said, "And if that place disappears, then all the magical beauty in our world goes with it. We will turn grey, like balls of mud, forgetting to read or jump or laugh or even to cry."

"I was older than you when I took the Red Book journey," Grandpa said, "Because the offer can only be made by the Keeper of the Secret to someone on the eve of their golden birthday. It's now or never. I don't know if you're ready, but I'm giving you the chance. What do you say?"

"Wow," the boy sat up on the couch and tilted a head in consideration. A precocious student, he was not prone to turn down challenges or fail to follow interesting paths. But this was serious business.

Without thinking, as if guided by a muse, the boy whispered, "Read the story."

Grandpa made an indistinguishable grunt, and the boy couldn't tell if it signaled satisfaction or dismay. But he went back to *The Land Between the Seas*, "Keep your wits, listen closely, and think in three dimensions. Over the eons, the True Name that preserved the magic was forgotten, a myth hidden by increasing layers of dust. Until the day a hero decided to go on a quest..."

- 2 - *The Oldest Man in All the Land*

Once Upon a Time, in the Land Between the Seas, **a brave human called William decided to go on a quest.**

It began with a dream. While sleeping he had a vision that foretold complete destruction for his world. Deep inside the Core of the Land, the stirring of an unknown force was causing a crumble. Creatures walking atop the Land could not feel it, but the crumbling would eventually reach them. When that happened, everything would fall with it.

In the dream, William was told that he was given information about the crumbling for a purpose—he had a role to play. The magic that turned Nothing into this beautiful paradise was fading. That's because remembrance of the True Name of the Land was nearly gone. If William learned the three parts of the True Name the destruction would stop.

William was a dreamer, and so he believed the story completely. He left straight away on his quest to collect the knowledge and save his world.

He first went to the universities and citadels to find the answer. He asked the wisest scholars for any information, but they knew little except that the world was *The Land Between the Seas*. None considered there might be a name older than that.

Undeterred, William the Dreamer then went to all the libraries and museums he could find. He asked the curators for information, and he read anything that might provide clues.

One hazy day on his quest, pondering on a green forest rock, William thought, “Who might know most about the oldest things, perhaps the oldest man in all the Land.”

What do you think, Listener on the Quest, is William on the right track? Our lives depend on you, so please stay vigilant!

That’s how the dreamer found himself tracking down birth records and asking town gossips about the most ancient elders.

He met with one man born a sixth of an eon before who said his friend was almost twice his age. He found that friend, a fourth of an eon old. That man said he didn’t know anything about a True Name. But he introduced William to a wrinkled tortoise of a woman who kept a list of ages for the record books.

That finally led him to the oldest man in all the Land, born more than half an eon before. His name was Abraham. The youngest of 16 children, he finally gave William what he’d traveled so long to find: important knowledge.

“The True Name of *The Land Between the Seas* has faded into near oblivion,” Abraham said from the rocking chair on his wood cabin porch. “But I remember. Some sang stories about the True Name. Three parts there are.”

At those words, William felt validation and hope. Abraham knew of the True Name. Three parts. Confirmation of his dream.

The oldest man shared all he remembered, "Long ago, two protected the Name—a Beautiful Turtle and Astonishing Snake. They were torn apart and each disappeared from sight. But they still roam. They must,” the oldest man explained cryptically. “I know what the three parts represent but I do not know what they are. Do you understand?”

The young hero nodded. *But did he actually understand?*

“The True Name of this magical place is a Shape. It’s the outline of the Land itself. The Shape can be said as a Sound. That Sound

has a Meaning. I don't know much more," the half eon old man slumped in exhaustion. "Best of luck on your adventure. I wish I could go with you, but I have my own quests here."

The grateful adventurer thanked Abraham and set off to share the good news. From town to town, city to hamlet, mountaintop to seaside, he told stories of his adventure. Thanks to the commitment to a dream, instead of being lost forever, generations knew that there was a True Name of their world, made of three pieces.

William the Dreamer's journey was a partial success. But the actual identity of the Shape, Sound, and Meaning remained unknown, the greatest mystery in all the Land.

- 2 - In the Living Room -

Grandpa finished the second tale with a Red Book riddle, "Dear Listener, your quest and our lives now continue with this question. Think carefully."

"An old man, a playful man, and an ambitious man walk into a tavern. Food and drinks are served, and after an hour only one man walks out. The tavern is then empty again. How?"

The boy blinked twice. He might have heard a riddle like it before, then remembered, "Because they are all the same person. An old, playful, ambitious man."

"Exactly! Even old folks like me are full of many qualities and hidden mysteries." Grandpa winked "You saved our world's beauty. For at least one more story."

THE 3RD TALE

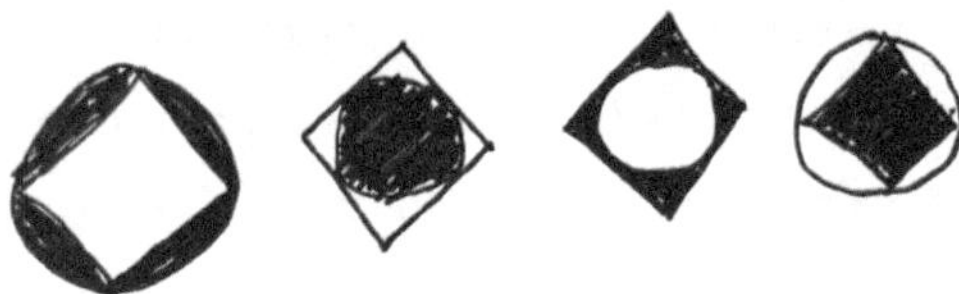

- 3 - In the Attic -

BOOM!

The century old hovering oak in Grandpa's yard lost a branch in the wind as I sat in the attic. It sent a tin roof echo down the house. I popped up from the crate, my head connecting directly with a wooden beam. The box burst open—the quarter dinged into a dusty shoe pile, the string spaghettied at my feet, the manilla envelope flapped up before landing hard, and the Red Book frisbeed into old clothes.

Had Zeus sent a Wake Up call?

I put the assortment back in the cardboard and remembered an old saying of Grandpa's. Whenever he solved a riddle he'd tap a finger three times to his skull, above an ear, and say, "Thanks to the 'ol box in the attic."

It was a favorite phrase—Grandpa's mind was his *'ol box in the attic.'*

"If you get in a sticky situation, remember to consult the 'ol box in the attic before making any decision," he'd say with three taps above the ear.

"The 'ol box in the attic is the most powerful computer in the world, did you know that? Right inside our own heads. It's the super secret hiding spot that we're each born with. The most complex object in the universe, except maybe the heart—but that's a lesson for later."

I exchanged the crate for a vintage lawn chair I found folded in a corner. The string, quarter, and envelope were back in the box. The Red Book lay on my lap, unopened. Part of me didn't want to crack the blank cardinal cover, worried I would ruin a beautiful memory by discovering the tales again.

Could a second reading ever compare to when I was 7 years old, sitting under a blanket, listening to Grandpa's storytelling, wondering if the world of magic was really on my shoulders...

- 3 - In the Living Room -

The Storyteller poured cereal for the boy on the couch in the blue slippers as they continued the Red Book quest.

Between spooning milk and crunchy bites, the boy asked, "How can a name be a shape? *The Land Between the Seas* is actually a shape?"

The old man shifted in his chair, the Red Book open to the exact right page, "Good question, it seems strange. But isn't a Letter just a shape? Watch."

As if waiting for this moment, the old man reached into a pocket and pulled out a long white string. He held it up by one end and wiggled it around like a snake dangling down from a branch. "Look at this. Some may think this is only a string, but others may see a line. There are always two ways to see everything."

He shaped the string into the letter S. "Look here, a letter is no more than a straight line twisted into a new shape. Everything is a shape. So maybe a name being a shape isn't too strange."

Rising from his chair, the Captain took the empty cereal bowl from the boy and handed him the string. "See if you can make letters out of this squiggly line of a string."

"That's easy," the basically 7 year old said from under the blanket. He took the string and curved it into the letter C. Then the boy flipped the letter into a mirror version to face the storyteller. "From where you sit a C would look like this," he said in a show of young brilliance.

"Excellent. C is a letter of utmost importance, especially to our family. It's the first letter of our last name and useful in so many words," Grandpa said with a shifty smile.

Prone to overachieving, the boy kept going and moved the string into an L. He followed that with a virtuoso performance of M, N, and P.

Grandpa stopped the string games with a mumble of interruption, "HmmmMmmm. If I may. I do believe we have a quest to attend to. I've been stalling," he admitted, "because I'm nervous about our journey. One wrong move and the whole thing goes. Be on your toes. The adventure continues now..."

- 3 - *The Feud of the Monument Shape*

Once Upon a Time, in the Land Between the Seas, creatures big and small found the deep well of magic hidden in their Stories. The discovery caused a great stirring to echo across all mountains, rivers, lakes, plateaus, and gardens.

Storytellers became the most sought after guests at any party, gathering, wedding, gala, and hoopla. They captivated eyes and ears with sagas of romance, mystery, and adventure.

One tale was by far the most popular—*The Legend of William the Dreamer.*

Over the eons, myths spread of the great hero from the past, William the Dreamer. Children learned of his exploits and quest for the True Name.

Schools across all rivers and gullies put on plays and performances of his journey. They crafted their own stories about the Astonishing Snake and the Beautiful Turtle. Their love, betrayal, and long search for one another was woven into minds throughout the Land.

The adoration for the Snake and the Turtle spread to adults who began throwing parties and then ceremonies around the Love of the Two Protectors.

In a dash of inspiration, one devotee proposed a large space honoring the Beautiful Turtle and Astonishing Snake. A building to showcase the best performances, a museum to house the greatest art, and a place for all admirers and scholars of the Legend of the True Name to meet, discuss, and create friendships.

The idea blossomed and soon planners brainstormed design ideas for the new arena. Ten of the best building artists were chosen to draft and present the final proposal. They hashed away at the monumental task. Everyone eagerly awaited the reveal. It would be the largest structure in *The Land Between the Seas*.

Celebrations were held in all nooks and crooks during the deliberations. Until finally the ten builders emerged, straightened their robes, and stated to the Land—"We are hopelessly deadlocked."

Five committee members believed the shape of the grand structure must have 4 sharp points, at the top, bottom, and sides. Some call it a Diamond. While the other five insisted that it must be rounded, curvy. Like the shape called a Circle.

Debate raged and everything between the seas boiled and rumbled in sound and yelling and stomping about the correct design.

During this explosion, a curious shift occurred. One word changed and the Land was never the same.

Before the Great Monument Disagreement, everyone participated in rituals for Turtles *and* Snakes. But during the Shape dispute the appropriate phrase became Turtles *or* Snakes.

Never forget, Listener on the Quest, even a single word can wield enormous power.

In less than a breath, all creatures in the Land shifted into either a Turtle or a Snake, but *never* both.

Turtles supported the Diamond design, while Snakes were for the Circle. Each side soon realized they disagreed on other things as well. Turtles preferred Numbers while Snakes were for Letters. Snakes prioritized leisure time and Turtles enjoyed nothing more than a long day of productivity.

The large arena honoring the Two Protectors was never built.

Forevermore the Land was divided between those devoted to the Beautiful Turtle and those committed to the Astonishing Snake. But *never* both.

- 3 - In the Living Room -

Grandpa pulled out another small book from his travel bag, this one filled with empty pages. The old letter writer always had a fountain pen on hand. He carefully copied a sentence from the Red Book for the boy now sitting up on one side of the couch.

Today his letters were sharp, an R with straight lines and a C with points at the top and bottom. The boy thought of this version of Grandpa's handwriting as "Vampire Letters," because some letters looked like they had fangs.

The Storyteller then asked the riddle from the Red Book, "Listener on the Quest, please don't fail us. If you answer this correctly, the page for the next tale will appear. Remember the story. "**What do the three circled words in this sentence have in common?**"

Snakes like tin cans for
they are circular & round,
So the turtle ate every
can he ever found

The old man stared at the Listener with raised eyebrows.

Think think, the boy encouraged himself. Remember the story. It was about the the Land being split in two. Turtles prefer numbers and Snakes like letters. But before that, everyone enjoyed both. *Snakes like* ***tin*** *cans* ***for*** *they are circular and round, so the Turtle* ***ate*** *every can he ever found.*

Eureka! The boy shouted, "The three circled words each sound like a number! Ten, Four, Eight."

"Correct," Grandpa smiled pearls and nodded. "Onward."

THE 4TH TALE

- 4 - In the Attic -

"A man with a heart three sizes too big. That's probably what killed him. Ha!" An ancient army buddy of Grandpa's said at his funeral from a wheelchair. It was a good joke, because the old man died at 100, anything could have taken him at that point.

It was only at his service that I appreciated how many people were grateful to have known him. Captain Robert C Cattrall had nothing if not an enormous heart. His war days were kept dark for me, but I heard whispers of his bravery, kindness, and showmanship.

In his later years he wrote that his three greatest achievements in life were once returning a trapped baby raccoon to its mother, helping his best friend Willy on a beach (whatever that meant), and being an example for me of living an authentic life.

He certainly did that, bouncing around the globe, hobbies big and small, friends near and far. I always felt he must be quite important, called away for work whenever emergencies arose. I never really knew what type of emergencies.

I once asked him the favorite place he'd ever visited in all the world. I wanted to tell my friends, because no one had seen more of the planet than my Grandpa.

He answered cryptically, "Hard to say, but the sound of the waves rolling into the shore is always something. Both beautiful and scary, don't you think?"

I never understood what he meant. *Do I now?*

- 4 - In the Living Room -

Smack!

The boy and his Grandpa high fived after he correctly answered the third riddle about words that also sound like numbers.

"Phew, that one is tricky for some people, good job little one," the Storyteller said as he stood in front of the couch with the Red Book open to the correct page in his hands.

"I wonder," the boy asked, "what about those who are deaf? How could they answer that question about words that sound like numbers? They don't hear sounds."

With a tilted head and twinkle in an eye, Grandpa said, "That is a mighty good question. I wonder if those who cannot hear with ears still have a sound that they make inside their own heads?"

He patted the red cover, as if in admiration, "I can't say for sure, the Red Book never reveals all its secrets, but I suspect it chooses riddles depending on who passes the gate. Every Listener on the Quest is different, with eyes, ears, and noses that work in unique ways."

The Keeper of the Red Book continued, "Did I ever tell you I was once temporarily deaf? As a young man, I found myself surrounded by the most earth-shattering bangs and booms. One was so close to me, my ears clammed up, ran inside my head, and refused to listen."

"Terrifying, I confess. It was only when I lost the ability to hear anything that I realized how much I loved listening. I wandered aimlessly in complete silence. I saw lips move but heard no words. I wondered how different it would feel to be born never knowing sounds, compared to losing the ability in the middle of life."

"During those silent hours, I remembered all that I once heard—my mother's voice, the buzz of a passing truck, boots on the ground, the different ways to laugh. Remembering a sound is not the same as hearing it again."

Transfixed, the boy threw off the blanket and sat upright on the couch. He had never heard this story from the old man.

"I read once," Grandpa looked at the Red Book, as if talking to it, "that there is no sound in space. Dead silence. In those hours after the booming scared my ears, I felt like I was not on planet earth. I went through the motions in this foreign land, pretending everything was fine, but inside I wondered if I would ever feel normal again."

"Then I heard it. A voice from nothing, 'Hey buddy! You made it! Great to see you here!' It was my friend, Mr. William Power from Virginia. He remains my most trusted confidant to this day. I still consider his words the most mesmerizing sound I've ever heard. "

"But enough of that. The quest awaits us." The Storyteller looked down at the pages of the Red Book and began the next tale...

- 4 - *The Search for the Most Beautiful Sound in the Land*

***Once Upon a Time, in the Land Between the Seas,* a young woman from the forests tried to mimic the birds that watched her from branches above each day. What came out was magic.**

Her songs became a heavenly siren, drawing in all the nearby flyers, transfixed by the delicate tweeting never before heard in the wandering woods. The birds were amazed to discover that it wasn't a creature like them that produced the beautiful melody, but a human woman.

The largest flutter of wings even seen in the Land gathered on the trees near the songbird, mesmerized by the performance.

The mass of birds did not go unnoticed by those in the towns surrounding the forest. A crowd soon grew around the young woman, and a chain reaction of curiosity pulled more and more into the woods. The Prince himself happened to be on horsey-

back nearby, and he too was irresistibly enraptured by the young songstress. It was Love at first sound.

Most consider it the first true musical concert in *The Land Between the Seas*. In the days to come, the young woman gave many performances, becoming the most well known vocal artist in the Land. She and the Prince remained madly in love, and she moved into the largest room in the castle. From a shy young woman of the woods to a Princess.

Two devotees of the Astonishing Snake, definitely *not* the Turtle, were at that very first concert underneath the tree canopy. Inspired by the singing, they had a Eureka idea—why don't they search for the most beautiful sound in all the Land?

As experts on the myth of the Protectors, the scholars knew that one of the three missing pieces to the True Name legend was the Sound of the Land. Wouldn't it be the most beautiful sound?

They set off on an adventure to find it. A quest like the one that you are on now, Listener to the Red Book. Use your ears, eyes, and voice to keep us safe. Preserve the magic.

Starting high, the devotees to the Astonishing Snake listened to the whirring winds from the pointiest peaks. They heard the caw of the eagles as big as apple trees that flew above the clouds. They went running from the piercing squeaks of the skinless stump bats hidden deep inside caves.

The rustle of the long grass on the plains gave goosebumps. The waves crashing against the sands were hypnotic, especially when combined with the sucking sound as the waters pulled back before charging in again.

The two on the hunt for the most beautiful sound in the world listened intently to the cling, clag, and clatter of busy streets inside the largest cities. They laughed with the villager said to have the funniest giggle in all the Land.

But after hearing what they thought was every interesting sound possible, they'd made little progress. They couldn't agree on the winning tone. One devotee preferred human sounds, while the other was drawn to the sounds of nature.

Just when they were preparing to return home, dejected after failing in their quest, they both heard it. A new sound that both felt instantly was the most gorgeous imaginable. It came from deep in the woods, a voice above the birds, a mixture of indescribable love and deep sadness. They followed their ears, past tree trunks of all sizes and leaves larger than whales. In the middle of the dark forest they discovered the source of the beauty.

The former songbird, once Princess now Queen, had returned to the spot of her very first performance. She sang alone to the slivers of golden light that broke through the canopy and lit up the open forest floor.

They discovered that the former Prince now King was missing on a dangerous mission, and the Queen felt an irresistible urge to return to the place where they first met. She wept as she sang, wondering if she would ever see her deepest love again. But she never lost hope. Her song spoke of a devotion she knew could never fade, even when the King was far away in mysterious reaches.

From that day forward, all those on the hunt for the True Name visited that legendary spot in those woods, hoping to hear the weeping love song of the hopeful Queen. Legend holds that it might contain a secret to the true Sound of the Land, if only the right ears could hear it.

- 4 - In the Living Room -

The next challenge was a test of sound. Grandpa's cheeks grew rosy as he finished reading from the book, "And now Listener on the Quest, to advance to the next story and save magic for your world and ours, please use your voice. ***What does the caw of the eagles as big as apple trees sound like? Then mimic the squeak of the stump bat coven. If you are close enough, we are saved.***"

"That's not a riddle!"

"It's a test," the old man explained to the boy. "The Keeper of the Red Book must be versed in everything about the Land, including how it hits the ear. It's either meant to be, or it isn't, I'm afraid. Be yourself and do your best."

The boy knew if he waited too long, he'd lose nerve. He trusted his instincts and....

Caw CawCaw CawwwAwAW! Squeeeel Squee Squeeeak!

Grandpa listened and stared at the book. He said nothing. The silence was painful. Still nothing. The living room remained church quiet.

Until...

"Bingo!" The Captain finally saw the page numbers to the next tale appear in the Red Book. "You've done it, m'boy!"

The 5th Tale

- 5 - In the Attic –

The multicolored straps on the vintage aluminum fold up chair pinched my back as I sat in the corner by the window. To relieve the sting, I got up and took a lap of the space. A storybook walk up attic, it felt more nostalgic than spooky, every object a memory from a past long gone.

I saw a battered notebook on a pile, it was filled with pages of Grandpa's doodles. He was hilariously terrible at drawing, but that didn't stop him from creating little images all over letters, notebooks, and paper scraps.

He said it was a way to turn his thoughts into pictures. "Even if they don't look like anything special to you, those little drawings mean a lot to me."

I flipped to an image in his notebook, and in a strange coincidence, I remembered the very doodle from decades past.

"Is that supposed to be a robot?" I had asked as he scribbled childish shapes.

"Robot? My dear boy, this is a Woodsman, from fairy tales."

"What is a Woodsman?" I guessed a monster of dark forests.

"It's an old term for someone who works with the trees and knows the magical creatures who live among them. The Tin Man from *The Wizard of Oz*—on the search for a Heart—he was just such a Woodsman."

"Oh, I get it," I'd seen the movie a dozen times, and Grandpa had even read me the original book. As a child the Scarecrow was my favorite, the Tin Man was most mysterious, and the Cowardly Lion seemed like he'd make a best friend.

I looked at the Woodsman doodle, and the soft tinging rain on the roof lulled me into attic daydreams.

- 5 - In the Living Room -

Successfully through four gates, the boy now felt an experienced Listener on the Quest. Grandpa must have thought the same." Since you've made it this far, I can now share that the Red Book includes drawings. They are no better than my doodles, as if made by someone first learning to hold a marker. But they bear great meaning—curious, mysterious, and full of origin magic."

"But don't even think about taking a look at them. Only the Keeper of the Book can glance at them without losing their mind. If you somehow make it through this, then one day you will see."

Grandpa paced across the living room, "Did I ever tell you that I like old stories, because I like to know the beginning of things. The core. That's a clue for you, Listener on the Red Book Quest."

"I've been thinking about the past a great deal today. It is one of those times when the mist of old memories catches up to you, the ghosts of legendary stories feel here again. Sometimes I go there in my dreams. It can be glorious to remember." Grandpa spoke to a corner. "But it's important to live now, not with yesterday's phantoms, because we never know what new magic the universe may have in store for us each morning."

"Learn from the past, enjoy it, but don't repeat it. It never ends well...

- 5 - *The Curse of the Unfathomable Monster*

***Once Upon a Time, in the Land Between the Seas,* a wave of nostalgia swept the world from coast to coast.**

It started in the middle of Timeless Lake, the largest ocean in the known universe. From there, it surged to shore, and soon everything about the past was in fashion.

One family of three brothers, devotees of the Beautiful Turtle, *definitely not the Snake*, decided to honor their favored Protector by embarking on the exact same mission as William the Dreamer—To find the oldest man in all the Land. Perhaps new knowledge could be gleaned about the True Name.

They followed William's exact path and to their complete and utter astonishment, they came upon a husk of a husk of a man rocking on the porch of a wood cabin. He mumbled, but they made out his name—Abraham.

This man claimed to know the original William the Dreamer. The three brothers thought that must be a mistake, because that would make him an unbelievable age. But with magic, anything is possible.

"I have a quest, I have a quest," this man Abraham kept repeating. The Turtle devotees assumed they would get nothing more out of him and were about to depart before the oldest of elders rose from his rocking chair and screamed what would become known as the Curse of the True Name—

You shouldn't have come. Retracing the past. Making me stay here for this.
Life is for new adventures. Original expeditions. Finding new bliss.

Now Darkness will come, an Unfathomable Monster will rise.
Changing everything that is, claiming the Land as Its prize.

Go collect your reward, for copying the past.
But you must know by now, that the glory will not last.

Delivering this Curse were the last words the oldest man to ever live ever spoke.

The three brothers rode back and shared Abraham's final words around campfires, kitchen tables, and city halls. *Was this man actually the very same who spoke to William the Dreamer?*

Word of their travels spread, bringing fame and great fortune. But it also brought deep paranoia throughout the Land. Children now learned of the Unfathomable Monster, a terrifying creature, indescribable, that lurked somewhere in the shadows, waiting to emerge.

This will not end well, dear Listener on the Quest, I'm sure you can see that by now.

Fear, distrust, and skepticism spread in some corners. One particularly nervous devotee of the Astonishing Snake blamed the brothers personally for unleashing the Curse and the Monster it predicted. *If only they had not gone on their silly quest.* In a blind rage, this man set fire to each of the brothers' homes.

The retaliation was swift.

The followers of the Beautiful Turtle used their superior strength to ensure Snake devotees would always be kept safely away, in a separate smaller half of the Land. Far more productive and strong than the romantic and storytelling Snakes, the Turtles became the undisputed leaders of *The Land Between the Seas.*

The legend of the True Name was no longer a story of Love between two Protectors. Flipped inside out, forever after it became a tale of a Curse and the lurking Unfathomable Monster—A story of Nightmares.

- 5 - In the Living Room -

The Keeper of the Red Book finished the tale, "Magic is about the mystery of the unknown. Life is about moving forward into that unknown, not getting stuck in the past. Now your riddle. You have three minutes to decipher this message."

Grandpa copied a message in the blank notebook and handed it over. "Your time starts now."

Sgnos evol dna niar eht ni ecnad SeKans.
Semoh tcefrep dna seitic egral dliub seltruT.

The boy wondered if it was an unknown language from the Land itself. He thought deep and believed he wouldn't be given a riddle he wasn't capable of solving.

Life is about moving forward, the Red Book said.

"Of course," the boy realized that the opposite of going forward is backwards. Dwelling too much in the past was like going backwards. The message needed to be reversed. The boy in the blue slippers bit a folded tongue in concentration and switched each word.

Songs love create and rain the in dance Snakes. Homes perfect and cities large build Turtles.

Close but not quite there. The whole message itself was backwards. So he flipped it, and read his answer aloud to his waiting Grandpa.

Turtles build large cities and perfect homes. Snakes dance in the rain and create love songs.

"My smart little golden birthday boy. You've done it again!"

The 6th Tale

- 6 - In the Attic -

Would the stories feel the same when I opened the Red Book again?

Those tales were a favorite connection to Grandpa Robert Cattrall the Showman and Storyteller. There is no way my reading could compare to how he delivered the charmingly curious book to an eager 7 year old the day before his golden birthday.

I wove the string from the box between my fingers. Then I picked up the Quarter, stared at George Washington, and tried to remember every president up to Lincoln. I used to know them all in order, because the old man taught me.

Grandpa felt connected to America, not the politics but the people and its story. One of his running gags, whenever anyone asked his age, was to claim he was a CC. When he received a blank stare, he'd then say "Calvin Coolidge was President when I was born."

It rarely drew a laugh, but he didn't mind. It was an inside joke with himself. Some old buddies called him CC, but that might have stood for something else, like Captain Cattrall.

Grandpa treated special pairs of letters as if they were tarot cards. Double letters were good luck, he said. He preferred some letters to others, as if they were characters in a story. C was a favorite, of course, followed by L, E, A, and P. I have no idea why. He might have been joking, but the old man claimed letters were magic when understood by a fluent reader.

With his love of letters and stories, if he was in *The Land Between the Seas*, he'd probably be a Snake. Though with his beautiful mind, he was also part Turtle. Maybe he was the extra rare blend of both.

I looked down at the Quarter I held in my hand, a coin the old man kept in his pocket all his life. It had a blue star drawn on the back...

- 6 - In the Living Room -

Grandpa delivered a mid-morning snack of water, ruffle chips, and apples with peanut butter. Thinking about the stories from the Red Book, the boy blurted, "Did you know that the Romans used letters for numbers?"

"Ah yes, Roman numerals." Grandpa sat with a handful of chips. "I suppose the line between letters and numbers can be complicated. I once owned a Roman coin. Augustus Caesar was on the front. But I traded it to a friend many years ago for a comic book."

The boy could not tell if this was a joke. Grandpa rambled after devouring an apple slice with an enormous peanut butter dollop, "I wish I could have a coin with CC on it, 'ol Calvin Coolidge, but they don't exist, so I settle for this."

He pulled out a regular quarter like the boy saw every day and artfully twirled it between knuckles. "At least it's good luck." Grandpa said, "And magical."

The boy was about to ask a question, but was stopped by the old man, "I can't explain more. You'll figure it out when the time is right. If by some miracle you make it to the end of this quest, then one day you might feel the luck of this token for yourself.

"Can I see?" the boy asked, popping off the couch.

Grandpa held the Quarter in a palm, Washington up. He flipped it over to reveal the usual American Eagle holding olive branches. The boy saw the national motto, *E Pluribus Unum*—Out of Many, One.

But it was no normal Quarter. Across the entire back was a hand drawn star in blue.

"Marked by the stars, this one," Grandpa said proudly. "As I said, you'll figure it out."

A palm snatched closed, and the Keeper of the Red Book put the magic quarter back in his pocket. "Coins can be much more than they seem. They hide messages and meanings."

Grandpa was on his favorite subject, American history. The boy ate an apple slice as the old showman explained, "The motto reminds us that when united, our differences are our strength. The sum is greater than the total of the parts. But coins are only as good as the trust that backs them. Otherwise they are useless pieces of metal. Never forget that."

"Now the blue star, that is something altogether more important. It's a personal symbol. A hidden message between those in the know."

"It's a hint to the next step on your quest. Be brave, young Listener..."

- 6 - *The Sage and the Hiding of the Magic*

Once Upon a Time, in the Land Between the Seas, **the Green Sage roamed the hillside near his village looking for mushrooms.**

He lived in a large community of Snake devotees. They spent most of their time cooking, gardening, singing, and practicing their favorite arts.

The surrounding land was a field of grass mounds, four men high and eight men wide. The Sage walked up, down and over each as he scoured. Until one of the mounds moved.

At least that is what he told the villagers he met as he tottered back to share his story. The Sage made the unbelievable claim that the mound was alive, sunken deep into the dirt below. The wise man thought that the mound tried to talk to him. But the moving hill of grass might also have wanted to eat him, and so the sage fled in terror.

The story would have ended there, a quaint local monster myth. But fate had more in store.

The Land was changing. For reasons that no one could figure out, a dullness seeped into parts of the countryside. Colors faded. Business stalled. Fruit grew smaller. Leaves didn't grow on trees. Artists lost their muse. Dancers couldn't find the flow.

The most learned scholars scoured ancient texts looking for answers and explanations. Some believed it came from the core of the world. Others blamed monstrosities deep in the darkest lakes.

Watching the fading around him, the Green Sage of the moving mound wondered—*Could the cause of the dullness be connected to the myth of the True Name?* The tale was not known by most any longer, but the Green Sage was one of the few who remembered.

You should know all about the True Name, Listener on the Quest, because discovering it is also your challenge, the only way to save us.

The Green Sage decided that his Mound experience was a hidden message that he must pursue. Collecting his courage, the brave wanderer went back to the spot where he first felt the earth move.

Almost immediately, it happened again. The same grass Mound shifted, grumbled, and began to rise out of the dirt. The Sage held firm, and waited for what came next. The Mound grew and the Sage saw a mix of scales, skin, shell, and more textures than he understood. Most of the creature remained underground, and the Mound itself might have only been the tip top peaking above.

It made a series of gurgling sounds, before forming words that the Sage could understand.

It's voice was deep and wonderous, "Trust your instincts. The remaining Magic in the Land must be hidden before all memory of the True Name disappears. Otherwise everything astonishing and beautiful will be lost forever."

Returning to the village, the Green Sage shared his story. He claimed the Mound taught him how to extract whatever Magic was left from each part of the Land and hide it somewhere safe. The method was a secret that only he could know, the Sage said, but he was up to the challenge.

It worked.

The Green Master and his fellow Snake devotees gathered all the Magic they could and placed it inside an object that represented them.

Followers of the Beautiful Turtle soon heard the story and did the same. They chose an entirely different hiding spot for all the magic their side possessed.

The remarkable objects were protected over eons, until eventually their existence was forgotten altogether.

That is how all the Magic in *The Land Between the Seas* was saved, but then lost—locked forever in objects few ever knew, and now no one does.

- 6 - In the Living Room -

The Red Book continued with its question. "The Keeper of the Secret must have a strong connection to the Land. Do you know what happened, even if it's not in the story? ***If one group hid their magic in a coin of solid metal and the other in a twine of ultimate flexibility, which group chose which?***"

Without glancing up, Grandpa said, "The ball's in your court, m'boy."

Back on the couch, the almost 7 year old was grateful it was a 50/50 question. Maybe even a guess would work. But he'd been paying close attention to the stories, and he put it together. A coin was like a shell, sturdy, logical, numbers based. The twine was a string, versatile, able to transform into anything, like letters and words.

He answered calmly, "The Turtles hid their magic in the coin. The Snakes put it in the twine."

Grandpa nodded. "Yessirree. You're getting the hang of this! The journey continues."

The 7th Tale

- 7 - In the Attic -

Grandpa treated his Red Book reading as delicately as open heart surgery. He explained, “I must say each letter in just the right tone. Every fluctuation matters. If I mistake a single word, then the gate snaps back shut and the book goes silent.”

The stories were not long, but Grandpa performed each at a careful pace. For some tales he took extra caution, running a finger under every word as he read, like reciting an incantation. For others, he almost danced around the room, a one man Shakespearean production.

I saw a stack of maps in an attic nook and it reminded me of his travel. But even as a globetrotter, he always kept roots at home with membership in every organization in town. If a secret club existed, I’m sure he was part of it. He couldn't walk down the street without bumping into Jimmy SuchandSuch from the SuchandSuch society that had a question about SuchandSuch. Tale older than time.

The former army Captain wasn't in the service too long before landing a government job traveling to disaster areas. As a proud grandson, I interpreted that as him being a secret agent, called in for undercover missions when the stakes were the highest. Of course he kept it all invisible, for the safety of the family. But I like to think he sent me hidden messages about the truth. No one ever proved me wrong.

He and I had secret codes with one another. The old man once told me "Codes are like signs in baseball. It's sending a message to someone, in front of someone else, but only the two of you know what it really means. Like an inside joke..."

- 7 - In the Living Room -

Another correct answer! The boy was in high spirits as a lunch of grilled cheese, grapes, pretzel sticks, and cookies was served.

That one seemed easy, though he tried not to boast. Once you learned a little about *The Land Between the Seas* it was obvious. The admirers of the Beautiful Turtle are probably the kids whose favorite subjects are science and math. The Astonishing Snake devotees likely prefer english and history.

The boy was about to mentally divide all the other subjects between the two groups, but Grandpa jumped in, "How're the sandwiches?"

"Delicious."

"Good good. Grilled cheese is a speciality. All about the timing, and the cheese to bread ratio. There are two trains of thought on that, but I shouldn't get into it now. We're on the biggest quest of your life, after all."

"Seems like there are always at least two different approaches to everything, know what I mean? In *The Land Between the Seas*, the Turtles and Snakes were night and day, mirror images of one another. That's probably why they started speaking different languages, or at least in very different codes. Some undercover specialists on each side even started using code names."

"Neat," the boy wondered if that was another of Grandpa's clues letting him know he was a secret government agent.

"Since we've made it this far on the Red Book quest, and you're almost halfway to becoming the new Keeper of the Secret, we might need code names. Just between us."

"Definitely," the boy agreed. His mind went to a Learning Channel show on "Famous Writings" about the *Gettysburg Address* and *Romeo & Juliet*. That's why he suggested, "What about Lincoln and Shakespeare?"

Grandpa smirked. "Clever names. Am I Abraham because he's the oldest man in the world in the Red Book?"

"No no," the boy giggled, "it's because you love presidents."

"Quite prudent," Grandpa nodded at his budding spy with the code name, "But Mr. Shakespeare, we better march on. Still a long way to go on this adventure."

The storyteller provided background before jumping into the seventh tale. "Over time the walls between those committed to each of the Two Protectors of the True Name grew tall and rigid. The Turtles remained superior, building great cities and new tools for life. The Snakes lived totally separate, sticking to their stories, books, performances, and fashion.

"The two sides *did not cross*, and so important news was passed on in deepest secret. Always in code..."

- 7 - *The Missing Magic and the Red Book Race*

***Once Upon a Time, in the Land Between the Seas,* a monumental discovery led to what is now called the Red Book Race.**

Somewhere deep in the citadel stacks, a novice sage from a Snake stronghold made a strange discovery in a forgotten text. Long before, an elderly Master Alfred donated his diaries to the citadel library. The Master studied the famous event then known as the Hiding of the Magic.

Master Alfred made a strange calculation. Using census numbers, food charts, travel vouchers, lottery records, and unknown scrolls, he discovered missing magic. Even with all the wonder held in the secret objects, a large amount remained unaccounted for. *Where was this magic?*

The Master claimed to know the answer—a mysterious third group of New Protectors controlled the Missing Magic. They hid it inside a Red Book found tucked in a rustic woodland library built inside a tree trunk on the borderlands. This ultra secret organization of New Protectors claimed to represent a middle path, the old way, admiring *both* the Turtle *and* Snake.

Listener on the Quest, don't forget, there is often a third way. Three is a magic number.

Master Alfred's diary headline for the Red Book entry was marked "Urgent!"

The novice sage immediately began the code protocol to get this vital information to the front lines. If the Snakes could find this book first, it might tip the balance, and they'd no longer be the weaker half of *The Land Between the Seas.*

With trained speed, the sage crafted a message and placed it in the designated location. He then waited for the morning post. As previously practiced, he said his coded phrase to the postal carrier, "Today is a good day to get a letter!" The sage then whistled. The words indicated a secret message waited, and the whistle meant it was *Urgent!* The postman tipped his cap to acknowledge the message received.

The novice sage was relieved that he accomplished his job properly. But there was much he didn't know.

He didn't know that his message was only the start. It set off a chain reaction of hidden signals. The postal carrier said his hidden phrase to the flower shop owner, "What beautiful roses today!" and then knocked his knuckles on the counter to indicate *Urgent!*

That flower shop owner made a special delivery to an elderly woman while saying "Looks like you have a secret admirer today!" with three rings of the doorbell.

This went on for many more secret Snake agents until it reached the front lines. The Snake code was two parts. One happy phrase that used the word "today" signaled that a message waited. If that message was followed by a sound, then it meant *Urgent!*

The novice sage who discovered the secret also did not know that he was being deceived. The postal carrier who spoke to the flower shop owner wasn't a Snake at all, but a Turtle agent in disguise. After delivering his message, this undercover specialist shared the secret with the other side.

This set off a Turtle chain of coded messages. While the Snakes used happy phrases and sounds, the Turtles preferred codes with numbers and colors. That's why the secret spy postal carrier mentioned an even number above 6 to indicate a message was ready. He then threw in a reference to "yellow," indicating *Hurry!*

Down the line it went, with agents mentioning even numbers above 6 and the color yellow until it reached the front lines.

The race was on. Whose messaging system would work the fastest? Who could get to the Red Book first and gain firm control of the magic it possessed?

The Snakes had a head start, but even one weak link can break a chain. Halfway through the run of secret messages, a boy on a bicycle forgot to ding his bell to indicate *Urgent!* From then on, the Snake messengers did not know to move as fast as possible. They lost the sprint, and the Turtles arrived at the tree trunk library first.

They grabbed the only red book among the tiny rows of shelves in the woodland library and returned victors in the race for the missing magic. Most said it was inevitable, as their side was much more disciplined than the Snakes, who often lost themselves counting clouds.

But did the red book they found in the small collection actually contain the magic? Or was it a decoy? Did the mysterious New Protectors of the Old Ways find another spot to hide their Red Book?

To discover that, dear Listener on the Quest, you must make it further along. Please act carefully. We are depending on you.

- 7 - In the Living Room -

Grandpa took a deep breath and finished the tale, "Invisible messages are critical to keep the Red Book hidden. Can you uncover a secret phrase from the current Keeper of the Red Book? Right now, with no warning? That's your test. ***The Keeper of the Secret will write a coded phrase on paper. You must guess what is written without looking. Can you read his mind? Now. Go.***"

The living room was midnight silent except for the occasional rain pitter patter on the roof. The boy allowed himself one second of panic before he stared across the room and tried to get inside his Grandpa's brain.

With a tilt of his chin, as if unsure, the old man considered. He tapped the side of his head three times, just above an ear, looked at the boy on the couch, and then wrote down a phrase in his empty notebook.

"Your turn to guess m'boy. Think slow and hard. What did I write?"

Blue slippers wiggled as the young one shrank into a ball under the blanket. How could the boy ever guess from any number of words his Grandpa could have written?

The old man would not have left him stranded. He would have given a clue—a hidden message.

Then the boy remembered. Three taps above the ear. He knew what that meant and he smiled while answering, "The 'ol box in the attic."

"Oh my, you've done it again!" Grandpa flipped his notepad to reveal the words, in sharp handwriting...

the 'ol box in the attic

THE 8TH TALE

- 8 - In the Attic -

Why do ghosts hide in attics?

Odd thoughts floated in and out of my 'ol box as I sat on the strapped aluminum chair. I still hadn't started the Red Book— *Why rush the journey?* Instead I stared at my Grandpa's life accumulations surrounding me.

Why do ghosts hide in attics?

Because that's where we store memories of the past. Phantoms float where they are remembered, in our highest rafters.

My eye caught a stuffed fish attached to a board. The largemouth bass was a gift from friends. The old man wasn't much of a hunter or fisherman himself—a hidden bambi of an old soldier.

The fish reminded me of the time I visited Grandpa's house after my first nature documentary viewing. I experienced the harshness of life in the wild—lions and tigers and bears, Oh My!

Grandpa ensured I found a soft landing. He didn't lecture but talked about how he felt the same fear at going through the scariest parts of life's adventure. But he learned that everything blooms and then rests so that we can be awed once again by new flowers. Like the sun rising, then setting, only so that it can rise again.

- 8 - In the Living Room -

I'm a magician too, the boy thought after correctly reading his Grandpa's mind and guessing the phrase *the 'ol box in the attic* with nothing more than a hidden signal. Maybe everyone gains special powers of insight near their golden birthday.

The boy glanced at the string on the table and felt sudden pity for snakes. Snakes were the bad guys in many stories. The Red Book knew better, and snakes got a fair shake in *The Land Between the Seas*, even if they were underdogs. Maybe it was another animal's turn to be the villain in fairy tales. *Squirrels get away with too much*, the boy thought as he looked out the window and saw brown fur scurrying up a trunk with an acorn.

Grandpa interrupted the boy's daydreaming. "I love my lucky Quarter, because the Blue Star is a hidden message from a dear friend. But I also love the String because you can do so much with it."

He picked it up and stood in front of the boy on the couch under the fuzzy green blanket. With the skill of a practiced magician, he held the string out dangling from one end, then swung with a wrist to catch the other end in the same hand. In a flash he tied the two ends of the string together, creating a loop.

"Sometimes it's nice to start over. Reset. Become something new. Don't you think?" Grandpa said as his fingers worked. "Like going back to nothing." He then held up the tied string to show that it was in the shape of a zero.

"I always thought zero was an interesting number." He winked. The boy wanted to remember that. It might be a clue that he didn't yet understand.

Pacing the living room, Grandpa explained, "The String transformed into something else. It now has space in the middle. An inside and an outside."

The old man shaped the tied string into a square, then a triangle. Finally he twisted the middle, creating two connected circles. He turned it sideways and asked the boy, "Do you know what this shape is?"

The boy guessed from the couch, "A sideways 8?"

"Technically yes, but for those in the know, it means more. It's an infinity symbol. It means forever and ever. I like to think of it as creating Something from Nothing. Infinity from a Zero with only one twist."

"We all can reinvent ourselves and blossom into something new if we use the 'ol box in the attic," Grandpa smiled before continuing the quest.

- 8 - *The Mysterious Visitor From Another World*

***Once Upon a Time, in the Land Between the Seas,* a visitor from beyond the stars changed the universe forever.**

He came from your very dimension, Listener on the Quest. Exactly how he arrived remains a mystery.

This Visitor emerged from an unknown cave straddling the borderlands. Villagers started a rumor that he walked straight out of a shadow painted on the cave wall.

With a kind smile, calm voice, and simple message, the Mysterious Visitor earned the trust of the first inhabitants he met. He came from somewhere beyond comprehension and had a simple mission: To help them all remember the Astonishing Beauty of this Land they call home.

He took bountiful joy in exploring between the seas. "I may seem like an alien magician to you. But where I come from, you are the true mystics. Everything is more mysterious than you can possibly fathom."

He traveled and shared the same message, drawing large crowds eager to hear the lessons from "The Man from the Cave Wall."

When his fame was great enough, the Mysterious Visitor revealed that he harbored a secret—He was the *Keeper of the Red Book, Guardian of the Missing Magic.*

It's what allowed him to visit. The man spoke of "New Protectors" who hid a red book in a tree trunk library. But it was a decoy. The Red Book hiding the real magic was given the ultimate protection, sent to another dimension. This story is being read in that dimension at this very moment.

The Mysterious Visitor then changed *The Land Between the Seas* forever. As a gift for sharing the magic of the Red Book, he offered them one ultimate wish—*Anything Their Hearts Desired.*

A group was formed with equal parts Snake and Turtle to decide what wish to receive. No decision could be reached. How could they ever agree on one wish for the entire world?

The group was left with no other choice. They would each roll one-hundred-sided dice, and whoever landed highest would decide the Wish.

The random winner was the youngest man in the group, and in a fortunate coincidence, also the wisest member among them. He thought carefully and came up with a request that he hoped without flaw.

"Our wish is for everyone in the Land to find the life that is the perfect fit for them, bringing ultimate bliss."

A sly smile broke over the calm face of the Mysterious Visitor, "That might be arranged. You want this to be Heaven for everyone?"

No one in the Land understood the term Heaven, and so the Visitor asked, "How would you like to decide the life that is a perfect fit for someone?"

The group considered carefully. Perhaps everyone filled out a form that listed their preferences on all the important parts of life: Favorite foods, favorite afternoon activities, and more. Then the Mysterious Visitor could ensure everyone got their favorites.

Who wouldn't want to eat their most mouth-watering treat every meal?

But others wondered, who wanted to eat the exact same thing all the time? What about discovering new favorites? Surprises? A perfect life cannot be explained by a form.

Then there was the issue of children—how old before you filled out the form? Do most adults truly know themselves?

An elderly scribe suggested that each parent would decide the perfect life for their child, and it would go from there. But that drew shivers. *Absolutely not. Everyone gets their own journey.*

The wise young man eventually found an idea that fit. Friendship was the most cherished virtue in all the Land. A true friend was someone who loved another without any desire to change them. Harmony between best friends is as close to perfection as was known between the seas.

The young man suggested that at whatever age someone chose, every creature could secretly select their Truest Friends. He suggested, "it is those Trusted Companions—friends, relatives, favorite trees, clouds, invisible pals, and all in between who would then design their perfect life."

The Mysterious Visitor respected the decision. "Done. Once I return to my home beyond the stars, I'll think it into reality. Magic is quite something."

***The Land Between the Seas* was never the same. The Mysterious Visitor's promise was fulfilled. It started immediately and continued for lifetimes. The deepest friendships blossomed as never before. Laughter grew so plentiful it shook the leaves larger than whales. New games were invented, and old games were played once more. Colors vibrated, and sounds echoed more beautifully. Creatures of all shapes and sizes had their dreams come true.**

Memories from before this Great Reset faded day by day, harvest by harvest. For the first time in eons, the differences between Turtle and Snake seemed less important than living the gift of the Mysterious Visitor.

That which is most important is often invisible. Don't you agree, Listener on the Quest?

- 8 - In the Living Room -

Grandpa did not look up as he continued, and the boy felt this must be an important part of the quest. "The Great Reset of the Mysterious Visitor gave the Land a second chance. Split in two, each mirror side had the opportunity to take its unique qualities and unite again into something much larger than the sum of its parts."

"Listener on the Quest, a Hero was needed to ensure the Mysterious Visitor's gift was remembered and protected. From here, two paths emerge. You must decide which one we take."

"Path One follows the greatest **White Wizard** in the Land. Does he lead a crusade with his perfect understanding of magic to bring us to safety? Path Two traces **Best Friend Heroes.** Do they stumble into glory and embark on an adventure together that saves the Land?"

"***Which trail do we follow, the White Wizard or the Hero Friends?***

Grandpa looked up, "What is your choice?"

Inspired by the tale of the Mysterious Visitor, the boy knew to trust his instincts and follow his heart. If he was on an adventure, he would much rather be with a Best Friend than alone.

"Let's follow the Hero Friends. Two is better than one"

"*E Pluribus Unum.* Let's hope you're right, Mr. Shakespeare" Grandpa nodded. "Off we go..."

THE 9TH TALE

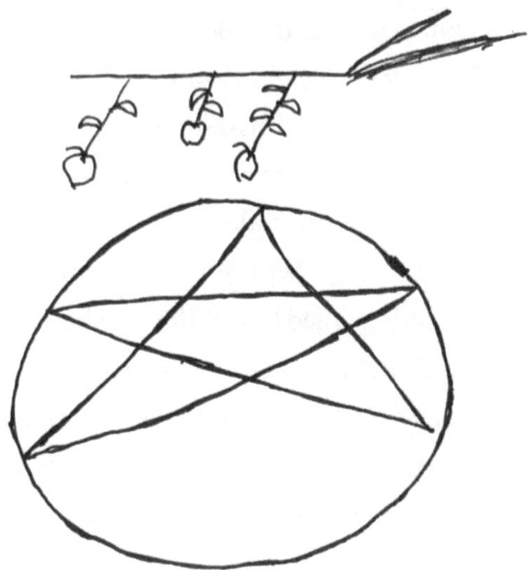

- 9 - In the Attic-

I looked at the Quarter with the blue star drawn over the Eagle and thought of the American motto etched above—*E Pluribus Unum.* It was one of Grandpa's favorites, because it fit so many of his stories. He said it meant, O*ut of Many, One.* United. That the sum is bigger than the parts, like the United States.

"Everything is connected!" he'd often say. "And don't forget that nothing matters more than the connection between people."

Friendship was his treasure.

"Nothing will matter more than the true friends in your life, dear boy," I remember his lecture. "*E Pluribus Unum*. Two true friends working together, when they become one, are worth more than ten strangers put together."

Sitting in the attic, I tried to twirl the Blue Star Quarter between my fingers like he could, but I failed. It slipped off my knuckles, and I had to crawl on hands and knees to grab it under a dusty dresser.

Looking down, I wondered, *who really drew that blue star on the coin*? If I was guessing I'd say the Quarter had some connection to Willy. If he ever started talking about friendship and the American motto, I knew a story with his buddy was about to follow.

His best pal all his adult life—Will, William, Captain Powers, among other names. Only Grandpa called him Willy, and he's the only one who called the old man "Bobby." He said they met somewhere in Nebraska, which seemed odd considered Willy was from Virginia.

The two seemed to super bloom as teammates. When paired at cards, they were unbeatable. Willy and Bobby won every 3-legged race they entered. Always the last two up cackling at late-night jokes, telling stories, and sharing deep discussions.

At least twice a week they'd order their favorite, Rudy's Pizzeria, the best thin crust this side of the river. The owner was a friend and memorized their order: One large—a quarter cheese, a quarter pepperoni, a quarter sausage, and a quarter supreme.

Sometimes they would burst into uncontrollable laughter at the mere sight of one another. Usually when they hadn't been together in awhile. With a friendship that long, deep, and true they must have developed an invisible language.

Strange coincidence about Willy, he was also a CC, born the same year, exactly one week before Grandpa in late May. They had many joint parties over the decades. Each made it to 100 years old, a feat which the old man insisted on. He said it was because 100 in Roman Numerals was C, his favorite letter.

An even stranger coincidence is that I was here for Willy's funeral when Grandpa died. The two centenarians, born one week apart, died one week apart. Each lived the exact same total amount of life. Tied to the end.

- 9 - In the Living Room -

"The Best Friend Heroes it is. Fingers crossed that they end up saving the day. You made a bold choice, because White Wizards are hard to beat."

Grandpa tried to bolster the young one's spirit. "Sometimes the hardest riddles are the ones that cannot be solved. They are no riddles at all, but moments when a quest provides only darkness, requiring us to trust our hearts and dive in with hope."

The boy was hopeful by nature, and felt confident in his Red Book choice. Even if he should have picked the Wizard, at least he trusted the feeling deep in his chest, as Grandpa said he should.

"Before we continue down the path of your choosing, I wonder, have they taught you about Gemini yet?"

Blue slippers swung over the side of the couch as the boy looked at the old man in the chair and tried to remember. He disliked not knowing something that Grandpa asked him, but he had no idea.

"It's OK if you don't know yet, it's an advanced story. But you're clever enough to hear the basics, especially because you are one. Just like me."

I am one?

"Messages are hidden in the stars. The ancients saw shapes in the way those shining dots in the sky came down to them. One of those shapes were known as the Best Friend Twins, Gemini. After all, *gemini* means "Twins" in Latin. If you were born in the part of the year that we were, then you are considered a "Gemini." It's our sign. Not exactly a secret, but another connection between us," Grandpa clarified with a wink.

"According to legend, two young men with fancy names, Castor and Pollux, developed an unbreakable bond. They were not actual twins, but they had connected souls. Together they are known as Gemini—helpers from the sky, coming to aid those in moments of crisis."

Popping up from the chair with athletic legs, the Keeper of the Secret pulled out his blank notebook and pen before walking over to the boy on the couch.

He drew two straight lines, the number eleven. The boy knew that it was Grandpa's favorite number, but didn't understand why. Then the old man explained.

"Eleven, my favorite number because it can mean so much. It could just be an eleven, or maybe it's two ones. It reminds me of Friends—Two Ones standing together, making something much greater. Ones that add up to much more than 2, they make 11! *E Pluribus Unum.*"

Grandpa then drew a line at the top and bottom of the eleven, connecting them. "When the bond between these two is strongest, they unite, becoming something altogether different."

He pointed at the new shape, "That is the symbol for Gemini, a sign from the heavens that you and I share."

"Time to march on. The world of magic depends on us. Or I should say, You!"

- 9 - *The Identical Strangers Meet The Bad Luck Boy*

Once Upon a Time, in the Land Between the Seas, **a rare horse-like creature with a coat of primary colors wandered into a mud bog and found himself hopelessly stuck. It was an accident that changed the Land forever.**

The mystical creature bleated and screeched in hopes of help. Luckily the bog was near a valley town. Two young men working on different sides of the village heard the distress call. One man was a Snake devotee and the other a Turtle descendant, but those differences mattered less and less. Memories had faded in the eons after the Mysterious Visitor's gift of a Great Reset.

With rope, brute strength, and teamwork the two rescuers saved the large beast's life. The mystical creature raced into the nearby woods and returned with a branch of apples—A sign of immense gratitude that brought good fortune. The young men ate the apples together, traded stories, and discovered their similarities.

The two became immediate Best Friends. They lived life on the same wavelength, cultivating a shared curiosity, love of animals, kindness, bravery, and sense of humor. If one was not great at a

task, the other was exceptional. Each knew what the other was thinking. The pair fit like two hands clasped perfectly together.

Listener on the Quest? Do you know what it's like to meet someone and feel an immediate connection?

Villagers began calling them the Identical Strangers, though they did not look alike. The young man from the Turtle side was tall, with blond hair, incomparable agility, and a regal disposition. The Snake was dark haired, shorter but strong and jaguar sleek, with a dancer's balance.

One day, the Identical Strangers were at the docks when they came upon the most pitiful looking boy they had ever seen. Covered in filth and doing the dirtiest jobs on the ship, he nevertheless wore a huge smile as he mopped, scrubbed, and hauled trash.

The Identical Strangers learned the child was called the Bad Luck Boy. The chief deckhand explained, "The boy's parents disappeared in a monsoon. His aunt fell asleep and never woke up. His orphanage burned to the ground. His favorite cat ran away last week. He's been thrown overboard three times. A mast once crashed inches from his head. It's a miracle he's still alive."

The deckhand swiped a handkerchief and frowned, "And now the poor fella is about to lose his job on this vessel, though he doesn't know that yet. I have to do it, because the other guys won't work with him anymore. They don't want to catch his curse. Some say he's evil. All I know is he is always smiling and laughs a lot. He might be a good kid with the worst luck, but my hands are tied."

Later, returning from the docks, the two Best Friends saw the Bad Luck Boy walking by himself along the road, barefoot, everything he owned in a knapsack. They decided to walk with him.

During a travel break, while watering the horseys, the boy saw a sparkle under a creek rock. He dipped a hand in the cool brook and scooped up an ancient coin from an unknown past. A blue star

was drawn across the back. The metal pulsed in the boy's hand, as if secrets were trying to escape it. The Bad Luck Boy ran his fingers over the coin in his pocket the rest of the trip.

He told his travel companions that he is always grinning and tries to feel happy because that is the last thing he remembers his parents telling him before the storm took them away. "Smiling helps," the boy said as he pulled out the coin to look at it again.

As soon as they reached the borderland village of the Identical Strangers, his luck changed. The two young men loaned him a yellow pence to play a carnival game. He won, and used the winnings to buy painting supplies. Some art he gave away, others he sold.

His reputation grew. The Queen saw one painted sunrise and insisted on meeting the artist. At the meeting the Bad Luck Boy pulled out the coin and twirled it. The Queen saw and knew it held great power. Out of greed and spite, she pretended to be sympathetic and adopted the boy, allowing him to move into the castle.

Her plan was to lure him inside, throw him in the dungeons, and take the coin. Luckily, the very day he entered the castle, the Queen slipped while on her morning walk. She fell into the moat and disappeared. She resurfaced through a dark brown pipe later in the day, but she'd lost the crown from her head. That meant, according to the rules of the kingdom, she was royal no more.

In a shock to the Land, by adoption, the Bad Luck Boy had become a Prince. And then with the Queen's fall, almost immediately the King. The Boy twirled the coin in his pocket as they put the crown on his head. From lowest deckhand to highest ruler.

The Identical Strangers were now known as the ones who discovered the new King. Forever after the pair were called the Twins, even though they were not related. In the *Land Between the Seas*, the universe always connects those who are a perfect fit.

- 9 - In the Living Room -

"Dear Listener on the Quest, if the Hero Twins have any hope at saving us, it's because of the magic, wonder, and beauty in deep friendship. Do you understand hidden connections with other creatures in your world? ***To keep hope alive, pick the 5 words from this list that belong.***"

Grandpa copied the words into his blank notebook and passed it to the couch.

Romeo	England
Amsterdam	Triangle
Curious	SpringField
Mary	Football
Hollywood	Honest

Quick on his feet, the boy stared at the ten words, trying to find the connection. *Which 5 belonged and which five did not?*

Think, think, think, the boy mimicked Winnie the Pooh, urging his brain to figure it out. So much depended on it.

Eventually the word Romeo was the giveaway. His secret names with Grandpa were William and Abraham. Shakespeare and Lincoln. Which 5 words were connected to them?

Romeo and England were definitely Shakespeare. Lincoln and wife Mary lived in Springfield. The final word was harder, but then it came to him, Lincoln was known as Honest Abe.

"Romeo, Mary, England, Springfield, Honest. Those five words belong, because they connect you and I."

"My Grandson is a genius," the old man belly laughed. "Correct! We march forward!"

The 10th Tale

- 10 - In the Attic -

I couldn't delay opening the Red Book forever. Eventually I'd re-read the stories, and try to remember the magic. If only because it's what Grandpa wanted. He left the manilla envelope that said "Only Open After Finishing the Red Book." They must go together.

I usually delay gratification as long as possible, a characteristic I'd had since a boy. If I could reap a greater reward by waiting, I'd be happy to wait. Though sometimes it feels like life is all waiting. Many of my favorite friends are the exact opposite. They go for things straightaway.

Grandpa was the master of relationships with people of all sorts. Unlikely friendships were one of his many specialties.

At his funeral an old buddy recounted the story of how Robert Cattrall, the Bobcat, was able to diffuse the most intense feud in the history of town. Two competing families of apple growers were mortal enemies since as far back as anyone could remember. If a relative from one side ran into someone from the other, trouble inevitably followed.

It was impossible to be friends with both families at the same time. Everyone picked which side of the apple growing dispute to support in the neverending social battle. With one exception: Robert CC Cattrall. My Grandpa somehow befriended both families.

Without telling either, he invited the patriarch of each clan to a cabin trip at the same time. No one knows exactly what the 'ol Bobcat did or said. But by the time they arrived home, the feud was over. The families joined forces and their apple venture boomed beyond dreams.

The apple families gave Grandpa the stuffed fish that ended up in the attic as a Thank You gift.

- 10 - In the Living Room -

Popcorn, pineapple slices, and apple juice served as the afternoon snack. The boy ate handfuls, because the quest took more energy than expected.

After draining half his apple juice in one gulp, Grandpa started a ramble, "Since the Red Book is on the topic of friendship and heroes and whatnot, have I ever told you about my favorite American friendship, Jefferson and Adams?"

This sounded like a topic the boy would have heard, but he didn't remember the exact story. He knew Grandpa would explain.

"John Adams and Thomas Jefferson, our second and third presidents. Legendary Founding Fathers. Once close friends who shared a love of books and knowledge, they became mythical enemies. Each had entirely different ideas about the future of the country."

Grandpa paused to finish his apple juice.

"Until the final quarter of their lives when everything changed. A mutual friend brokered a truce, and the two old lions started sharing letters to one another, re-building their bonds. Those messages are now some of the most important words in our American story."

The boy shoved in a handful of popcorn, captivated.

"It gets even more interesting," the Captain said from the chair. "Both men died on the exact same day. Weird. And guess what day that was?" He did not wait for an answer. "The 4th of July, on the 50th anniversary of the Declaration of Independence, a document those two men wrote and edited together."

"What a strange coincidence. Now on with the quest..."

- 10 - *The Hero Twins Discover the Girl Split in Two*

Once Upon a Time, in the Land Between the Seas, **a desperate father went on a search for two young men known throughout the countryside as the Hero Twins.**

The man's daughters were fading and he heard that the Twins possessed the rarest good luck magic. Storytellers spread the tale of how each consumed wondrous apples after rescuing a trapped horsey beast. Best Friends with kind hearts, the Heroes were said to come to the aid of those in dire situations.

Scouring the borderlands, the father wandered until he found the Hero Twins village and begged their help.

Swayed by his plea, the pair left straightaway to the father's hamlet. As they traveled the grateful parent asked the Twins their names. Laughing, both admitted they forgot their old names, since they now acted as a unit. But in their village the tall blond Turtle was known as Twin A, and the strong sleek Snake was Twin B. The father agreed to call them A & B, easy to remember.

Before they entered the house, the desperate father stopped the Twins to explain the details.

"One moon cycle ago, my daughter Mary was struck by lightning in a sudden electrical rain. The bolt split her completely in two. She survived, but became two people, Mary & Mary. Once you get over the look of a half a person, you can see that each side is normal but particular."

He gulped then continued, "The Marys are mirror opposites of one another. They agree on nothing. I suspect it's because each took half of everything—half a heart, half a brain, half the strength in each leg."

"I'm so sorry to hear that," Twin A offered a sympathetic smile.

"The real difficulty is that each Mary is now fading. It's only a matter of time before they're gone. They aren't meant to survive separately. Our only hope is to stitch them back together. We have a healing professional ready to do it. But there's a problem."

"A problem?"

"Each Mary refuses re-connection. They say they'd rather fade away than be sewn together with someone so different from themselves. As Hero Twins, even if not by blood, I hoped you might be able to help?"

"We can't make anyone do anything, but we always try our best," the pair said in unison.

The Heroes approached the house and noticed a group of children singing together next to a window. They held hands in a circle and called out, "Mary Mary, quite Contrary! Why do you argue so?"

The Marys were under covers up to the neck on each side of the room when the Twins finally met them. The sisters lay bedridden, walking took too much energy since their fading began.

The two bickered for an hour as the Twins listened. If re-connected they would fight about what to eat, which stories to read, trips to take, and who to call a friend. Since the lightning strike, each Mary had grown separately. That freedom was impossible to give up. The only thing they agreed on was that they were no longer a good fit together.

The Hero Twins used their power of combined persuasion to change minds. They understood the Marys predicament, but per-

haps something more could bloom from the connection. After all, Twin A and B were from opposite clans, very different, but together became something much more.

Just perhaps, the Hero Twins wondered, the Marys could become a team, with everything they'd learned separately, they might transform into something extra special. Besides, if it was too unbearable, they could always unthread the stitches and separate once more.

The Hero persuasion worked, and the Marys agreed to a temporary connection. The result was magic. The duo forever after called "The Marys," became icons. When each half of The Marys brain was connected, she became far more brilliant than before. Her combined heart overflowed with love, kindness, and joy. Her two legs ran faster and jumped higher than she thought possible.

The Legend of the Hero Twins grew to new levels after they rescued The Marys. Stories of their exploits spread, and they became the most famous pair in the Land.

- 10 - In the Living Room -

"I hope you've been paying close attention, dear Listener on the Quest." Grandpa read from the Book. "Saving our world of magic is about finding connections between everything in the universe, even those that appear opposites. Can you spot this connection? ***What do the shapes in Row 1 have in common that those in Row 2 do not?***"

In what was becoming a routine, Grandpa copied down the riddle and walked the notebook to the couch. The slow process made the boy eager for a day could read the words directly from the Red Book.

Row #1 - M, H, A, 8, O, II

Row #2 - N, Z, 9, K, R, VI

"Hmm," he considered. Letters, Numbers, even the Gemini symbol. The Red Book tale was about mirror opposite girls that became something more when sewn back together.

Eureka! That's it!

The boy made a connection. Mirror opposites. If he held this notebook up to a mirror what would he find? Those in Row 1 would look identical, they are the same forward and backwards, in a mirror and not in a mirror. But the shapes in the bottom row are not symmetrical, in a mirror they are opposites.

He gave his answer to Grandpa and held his breath.

After a long pause the book finally revealed the pages to the next story. "Yes! Another correct answer." The Storyteller beamed from his chair, "We move forward now deep into the Red."

The 11th Tale

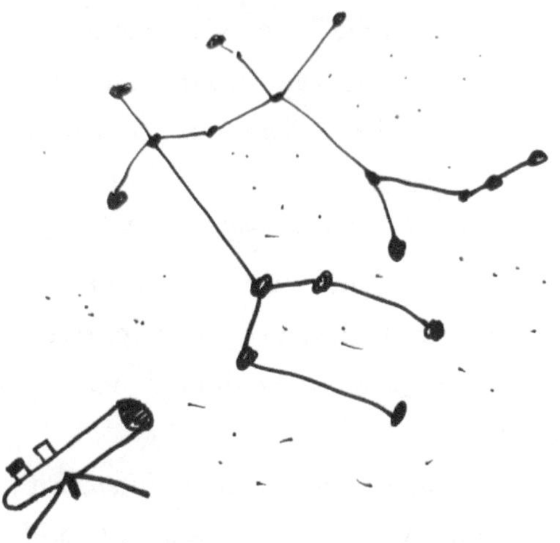

- 11 - In the Attic -

The rain on the tin roof lulled to a drip, and the sun emerged behind a cloud. Out the large attic window, I noticed another visitor in the sky—a white-silver full circle moon sat calmly in the soft blue. The sun and moon, together.

Grandpa bought a telescope for my birthday in middle school. I'd discovered astronomy and began thinking about the biggest questions in the universe. Going from watching the night's movement with the regular eye to seeing it through the magnification of the telescope lens was revolutionary. Tiny dots exploded into wispy balls of flame and fury in the murky galaxy. The Moon became an infinitely more complex orb with craters, crevices, and secrets hidden in its grey folds.

In those days, I impressed classmates by being able to find the Gemini constellation in the sky, pointing out the blue light pricks that combined to create the Twins. On the night of the telescope birthday, being my own sign, Gemini was the first constellation I saw. I scanned for the two brightest stars, the heads of the Twins, Castor and Pollux. Even though it wasn't the best season for it, I captured them straight away.

The magnifying eyes of the telescope transformed Gemini. No longer a flat connect-the-dots game, the shape of the constellation disappeared. Castor was big and bright with the regular eye, but the telescope showed that it was actually a *star system* made of multiple parts that only appeared as one from earth. Each star of the Twins seemed close together with the eye. But the magic telescope showed that they were thousands of light years apart.

It's all relative. Anything can look entirely different if you change your angle or magnification. An important lesson of Grandpa's that I could do well to remember as I grow older. I wonder if he has a telescope in this attic...

- 11 - In the Living Room -

"Now we've arrived at it," the Keeper of the Red Book Secret stood at attention. "The 11th tale. A number of extraordinary power. A joy to behold."

The almost 7 year old boy with the impeccable memory rolled his eyes, knowing the old man exaggerated about the silliest things, like a favorite number.

Nimble hands picked the string back up, and wove it through his fingers with seasoned expertise. "Did you know," Grandpa said as he fiddled, "that this snakey twine can make more complex shapes than letters and circles?"

Strong fingers worked as he explained, "Creating string figures is one of our oldest arts. The one I'm making now might be the most popular."

He wove shapes as some organization burst from the string, like a spider's web becoming a natural wonder strand by strand.

With a flourish and finish, Grandpa stretched out to show layers of a unique pattern. "Jacob's Ladder. It's the first one I learned. Have you heard the story of Jacob and his ladder dream?"

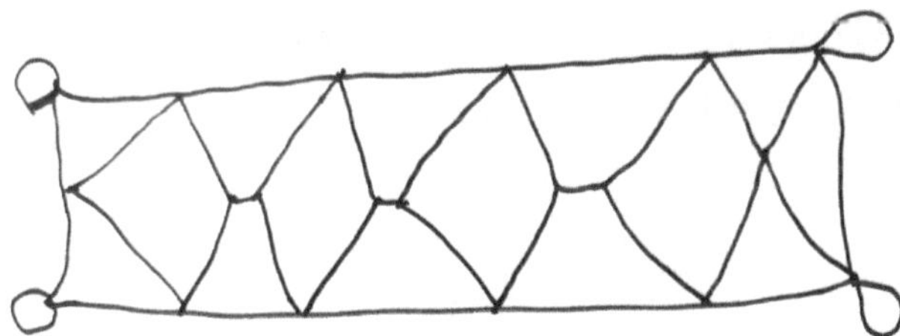

The boy had not and said so, knowing the old man wanted to tell the tale regardless. "It goes something like this: A fella named Jacob falls asleep and has the most vivid dream of his life. In it he sees a staircase to the sky. He climbs up and up and up. Into the clouds. Can you imagine the view from up there?"

Grandpa dropped the string ladder and it returned to an O shape. "While up high, Jacob realized he was surrounded on all sides by magical white creatures. Protection, to ensure he didn't fall. They wished him good luck and set him on some sort of journey. It all works out for him, I think. But the main point is that if you ever have a dream like that, then you're in for an adventure. But you'll have protection. Keep that in mind."

"I've never had the dream myself," the old man confessed, "though I have magical experiences of a different sort."

The storyteller leaned in close and whispered, "I'd never say this to anyone else, but since you are the Listener on the Quest, you deserve to know. Sometimes I end up in *The Land Between the Seas* in my deepest sleep. Dreams might be the only way people from our world can get there."

In an even quieter whisper, "And I think they can come here. If you look close at the sunlight bursting through twilight clouds or moonbeams across a still summer lake, you can grab glimpses of sleeping spirits from *The Land Between the Seas*, sneaking out to catch a glance at those mystical creations from their own sky, You and Me. "

"Ready or not, here comes magic number eleven..."

- 11- *The Two Quests to Save the Universe*

Once Upon a Time, in the Land Between the Seas, the King, once known as the Bad Luck Boy, found himself lost in the Endless Woods surrounding the castle.

A sudden leaf hurricane sent his party fleeing in all directions. When it finally stopped he was alone in the Nowhere with no idea how to get back home.

The King rested on a stone and hoped for a sign from the universe. He smiled as he drifted into dreamworld.

In the strange space between asleep and awake, the King heard a Voice coming from the Core of the Land. It told him that he'd soon find a way out, because he had a role to play.

The Voice from the Core shared the tale of the True Name of *The Land Between the Seas.* The world was healthier than ever before on the outside, but deep inside there was a fading. Memories of the True Name went extinct. Unless a Hero could be found to uncover the Shape, Sound, and Meaning of that Name, everything would be lost.

The dream became a nightmare.

"An Unimaginable Monster will rise at the end. All will shudder," the Voice from the Core said before the King woke with a rattle.

A breeze blew through the trees which ignited a piercing blue light gleam. The King walked toward it, wondering how moonlight could penetrate the Endless Woods in the middle of the day.

As he walked, the blue light kept moving forward, eventually leading him back to safety. The grateful King believed that the dream Voice from the Core saved him. He remembered every detail of the vision and immediately summoned the Land's two best hopes of uncovering the True Name—the Hero Twins and the White Wizard.

You remember choosing between these two, don't you dear Listener on the Quest?

The Twins, once Identical Strangers, helped the King when he was the Bad Luck Boy. The White Wizard was the beloved miracle worker of the Land, cherished by the downtrodden, brilliant beyond measure, and the King's most loyal aide.

The White Wizard mastered every book on the True Name myth, and started his quest. He searched for the Meaning of the Land, believing the most important part of the name should be found first.

The Hero Twins went the opposite direction. They thought that if they could identify the Shape, then the remaining two pieces should fall into place, one after the other. Sound and Meaning were misty concepts, hard to find by chance. But the Shape of the Land could be identified with skill, strength, and ingenuity.

Neither Twin A or B could figure out a way to the answer on their own. But once they sat and pondered together, a brilliant idea came to them.

A shape can change depending on an angle or perspective. Twin B realized that no one could figure it out while walking on the Land itself, but what if they changed the place from which they looked? Twin A knew exactly what he meant and what they must do next.

Climbing up the windiest peaks, they traveled to the highest spots where the last scraggy trees grew sideways over mammoth drops. There they found the stick crater nests of the eagles as big as apple trees.

At any moment the Twins risked a vicious crane claw or deadly beak bite, but they inched toward the monstrous flyers. With the bravery that made them famous, they asked the mountain soarers for aid in their quest.

"Eagles are here to help," the Chief said immediately, "but few have the courage to ask. Let's go."

With that the Twins found themselves the first humans soaring through the clouds atop eagles, in the heavens, observing the Shape of the Land from an entirely different angle. Twin A diligently sketched what he saw, and Twin B took everything into his deep vaulted memory.

When they landed, the pair were confident they knew the Shape of *The Land Between the Seas.*

But they decided to keep it secret, between themselves. Their notes were burned, and they took the Shape into memory. Some suggested it was a smart move to keep the Secret until all three parts were known. Others worried it was a trick, and that the Twins had no idea about the real Shape.

On the other side of the tall mountains, the White Wizard made progress and shared all he knew with the wide world.

A stark contrast grew between the two groups of adventurers.

The Land split once again. Now not between Turtles and Snakes but between those trusting the Wizard and those rooting for the Hero Twins.

- 11 - In the Living Room -

"You know the situation, potential Keeper of the Red Book Secret," Grandpa read solemnly. "We now offer you a Great Reset. One of these paths ends in ruin, the other in true victory. ***Would you like to continue following the Hero Best Friends as they try to discover the truth? Or is it time to switch to the White Wizard as he uses his unmatched powers to save magic?*** Decide now."

The boy hesitated only a moment before answering, "I'd never abandon my real friends. I'm sticking with the Hero Twins."

"Attaboy," Grandpa smiled as if the child had given the only respectable answer. "Let's go and win this thing."

THE 12TH TALE

- 12 - In the Attic -

Honk Honk Honk

Oh no, I recognize that sound!

A jolt coursed from skull to toes, sweat bubbled my skin, and I darted down the attic stairs. All from a sound.

A car alarm blared, and like a parent recognizing a cry, I knew it was mine. Maybe a cat jumped on the hood. Or perhaps Grandpa wanted me to stretch my legs.

After silencing the grey Audi, I looked around the yard. Not much to see except for his Memorial Day flag and a pink flamingo. Then I noticed the zen water fountain with three golden orbs running next to a bird bath. It was dry, rumbling a jarring whir of unoiled grinding gears.

I unplugged the gadget with a pang of sadness. The final sounds made by the trusty lawn fountain and the memories it held.

Sounds are strange. Like how a foreign language hits the ear.

Once on returning from a Rome trip, the old man gave me a miniature Colosseum. It sat on my desk next to a fish tank for the next decade. He also brought the strange sharp tones of the Latin language.

Captain Cattrall liked to get at the root of things, and so instead of learning Italian while traveling, he chose Latin. Tanned and lean after his getaway, he greeted me with a long bearhug, "My dear dear Amicus!"

He explained that *amicus* meant "friend" in Latin, though it sounded like something was caught in Grandpa's throat. Sounds are strange.

"The words of the great Roman Empire," he said before teaching me a few phrases that have taken up a permanent place in my 'ol box in the attic.

Amicus meant friend. A stranger was an *Alienus.* That one was easy, because I knew all about aliens from far away galaxies.

The only others I remember from the lesson are that *Melius* is better, *Peius* is worse, and *Optimus* is the greatest.

As a kid I found reasons to use those words so I could hear Latin in my own voice. It hit the ear like cotton candy, fuzzy and fun. For all I know his Latin might have been completely wrong. It didn't matter. Sounds are strange.

- 12 - In the Living Room -

Beep Beep Beep

The oven chirping reminded Grandpa to start the french fries. He strode into the kitchen with a yell behind him, "About thirty minutes until dinner, time for one more story. Hopefully not the last one."

He took the Red Book with him, and the boy was left to his thoughts. *Were the Hero Twins the best hope to save the Land, or should he have switched to the White Wizard?*

The boy stretched in his blue slippers until Grandpa returned. "I'll bring a plate for you once the fries are done. You'll need strength to have any chance of finishing this quest."

Sometimes Grandpa broke small rules that adults forced on little ones. On this special day the boy was allowed to eat from the couch, in his slippers, and wasn't jammed into the uncomfortable dining room chairs with a napkin on his lap.

Grandpa gave the menu, "For dinner, on top of the french fried potatoes, I will prepare for you a sandwich of your choosing. We have peanut butter and jelly. Turkey, ham, and swiss on rye with a hint of jellybean tucked in. Or a sourdough loaf stuffed with hot peppers, bologna, yellow cheese, and slathered in thick mustard."

"Eww, I hate mustard. You know that," the boy smirked.

"Of course I know that. It was a test to ensure it was the real you and not an imposter. I don't want an *Alienus* hearing a Red Book tale. It would ruin the whole endeavor!"

"Speaking of mustard," the Storyteller was on to his next topic, "Did I ever tell you about the time my old boss temporarily went blind? It was mustard's fault. Which is why I only use ketchup."

"Did your friend accidentally get mustard in his eyes?" The boy did not understand.

"Something like that, though the mustard was in gas not goo form. He was a tough fella, army gentleman, and able to keep calm even when everything went dark. The General said that when his sight went away, his hearing changed and he grew superhuman ears."

"General Maymerry could hear anything, bird tweets from faraway forests or critters scurrying a football field away."

Grandpa was standing again, Red Book in hand, in storyteller mode as he remembered his old boss who went temporarily blind.

"I am soft on my feet, but I could never sneak up on him. No matter where we were, before I got close, he'd call out, 'Hey there Bobcat, you're sounding good today.' Perfect hearing is a mesmerizing skill, and it made the General one of the most impressive men I ever knew."

Grandpa finished with a question that made the boy wonder, "I was jealous of his hearing, but then I remembered it came at the price of not being able to see. Would you risk going blind forever to get superhuman ears? Too scary for me."

"Number Twelve awaits. Close your eyes, listen, and try to save the world..."

- 12 - *The Great Race to Hear*

Once Upon a Time, in the Land Between the Seas, the two quests to uncover the True Name merged in what became known as the Great Race to Hear.

The legends of the age, the White Wizard and Hero Twins, found themselves on the same hunt to uncover the True Sound of this most ancient of worlds.

Everyone in the Land rooted for *some* champion to discover the answer, because their very existence depended on success. But each hoped that *their* favorite would be the One.

Creatures from the highest peaks to lowest caverns chose sides, speculated, and wished to the skies. Supporters of the Wizard wore white and green clothes, while fans of the Twins had a fondness for yellow and blue. Homes were decorated with the colors of each Hero. Flags flew from sea to sea.

Very different strategies guided the two campaigns to find the lost Sound.

The White Wizard was careful and comprehensive. He believed he knew the Meaning of the Land, and so he tried to understand the sound of the Meaning. Starting at the beginning, the master magician left no rock unmoved, reading every line of the oldest scrolls for any reference to the Sound myth.

An inventor without match, the White Wizard designed special earmuffs that magnified his hearing. He programmed the machine to provide a number based on how the sound made him feel. A low number was horrified, a high number was astonishing beauty.

The Wizard roamed the countrysides, prairies, fields, valleys, hollars, cities, villages, and everywhere in between. He dutifully recorded the scores of all that he heard through his magical muffs.

He had a particular fondness for the *Hush* immediately before a curtain was drawn for a performance.

But the wise magician had a secret idea. There was no reason that the sound had to be pleasant. Maybe the True Sound of the Land didn't bring joy but instead evoked fear to keep it most protected.

After wandering the darkest corners, slimiest crannies, and most desolate wastelands, the Wizard believed he found it—the most terrifying Sound in the Land. It earned a score of Zero, indicating absolute dread. The Wizard could only experience it three times before fleeing in terror.

He heard it in an abandoned house that stood alone in the middle of a soiled farmfield, built by primitive brawlers eons past in a grey place that saw no sun. The sound was a...

Knock Knock Knock
At Midnight
From inside the cellar door
Under the house.

A rumor soon spread that the **Knock Knock Knock** came from the Unfathomable Monster, announcing its horrible appearance.

On the other side of the world, the Hero Twins took an entirely different path to find the Sound of the True Name. They brewed a special tea and in a solemn ceremony asked the Universe to guide them to the Sound. The duo believed in destiny and fate.

Together the Twins A and B experienced a shared vision. A Voice from the Core told them to find the cave of a Mysterious Visitor. The True Sound of the Land could be heard inside but only by the most worthy of Heroes.

They didn't know the Legend of a Mysterious Stranger and had no idea where to find this cave. But that did not deter them. Champions of friendship, the Twins knew where to go, the smartest woman in all the Land, and a treasured *amicus*.

The woman known as The Marys was happy to help the Heroes. A renowned guru and scholar, she knew all about the myth of this Visitor.

"He came from the Keepers of the Red Book," she said. "Bringers of the Great Reset."

The Marys shared a rumor of a hidden mountain range, along the old borderlands, where legend claims a man emerged from a shadow on the stone wall.

The Hero Twins set off to this range. Searching with speed and prowess, they found a snake sliver of a cave opening in the hardest shell of the mountaintop. A strange blue light pulsed within. Stepping inside, they noticed the entire floor of the cave was covered in a pathway of black brick. Their boots made a **Boom, Bamb, Boom, Bamb** sound as they followed the otherworldly road to darkness.

The black brick road dead-ended at a deep chasm, blindness all the way down. Strange glowing mushrooms grew over the cave walls at that spot, surrounding the shadow of an enormous man burned into stone—The Gateway of the Mysterious Visitor.

Guided by fate, the Twins knew what to do. The Heroes echoed sounds down the deep pit and listened to what came back to them. They tried many combinations of words and letters. Until Twins A and B looked at one another with invisible understanding. Both suddenly remembered, and each said the other's *original* name down into the endless darkness.

A simple, clear sound sung up to them from the Core. It came with a magical breeze that coated them like dew. The Best Friends

felt most deep that what they heard back at them was the Sound of the True Name.

But as with the Shape, the Hero Twins chose to keep that sound secret, telling no one. Now they need only find the Meaning of that Shape and its Sound to save the world and fulfill their destiny. Failure meant all would be destroyed forever.

- 12 - In the Living Room -

"Listener on the Quest, there is little time left for deliberation. The Keeper of the Red Book must master all sounds, even gibberish melodies they couldn't understand and languages they don't know. Do you possess the gift? ***What do these sounds mean?***"

Grandpa then spoke words that seemed gobbledygook. Could he figure it out?

"Duo amici meliores sunt quam decem alieni"

The boy felt a pang of terror. *He had no idea. It sounded like nonsense!*

Until he took two deep breaths and the image of the Colosseum next to his fish tank popped in his head. Latin! He knew *E pluribus Unum*. But did he remember any of the others? He asked Grandpa to write it down.

In the blank notebook he wrote,

Duo Amici > Decem Alieni

The Storyteller had secretly given him a clue. Of course! The boy made the connection between the words Grandpa taught him and one of the old man's favorite phrases.

"Duo amici meliores sunt quam decem alieni"

"Two friends are better than ten strangers!" the boy yelled in triumph

"Amazing! Correct answer. Now let's eat!"

THE 13TH TALE

- 13 - In the Attic -

After silencing the car alarm, I went back to the box in the attic. On the way up I caught a flattering glimpse of my reflection in the hall. I thought I looked good for my age, but mirrors play tricks on us. I tried to remember what Grandpa looked like at this point in his life but couldn't nail it down. Memories are misty.

A few weeks before he went to whatever comes next, the old fella told me, "I don't know why I remember certain things and not others, or why some scenes in my life stay in the 'ol box and others disappear."

In another conversation Grandpa said, "Memories flood back at nature's pace. Trying to control it is like trying to prevent a summer tornado. Impossible to do, just gotta let it happen. Like falling in Love."

The Red Book of tales about *The Land Between the Seas* was ahead of its time, and must have been a choose your own adventure or fill in the blank story.

I now know Grandpa must have adapted it to fit me. I felt ready to open it again, to read the original tales. If only so I could see what was in the manilla envelope—"Only Open After Finishing the Red Book."

- 13 - In the Living Room -

"Maybe I have a golden grandchild after all," Grandpa congratulated his young ward in the blue slippers. But then said ominously, "Maybe you'll become Keeper of the Secret after me, unless you make a mistake and destroy everything forever."

A loud beep from the kitchen popped Grandpa from his chair, "I almost forgot, the fries!"

The boy shuffled off the couch and stared out the window. The rain filled rivers along the curbs, before disappearing underground into pipes big enough for boys to fit in. Thinking about hidden passages underneath town and what must lurk there made the boy shiver.

Grandpa danced back in with a plate in each hand. PB&J, fries, and applesauce—he ate the same as the boy. "Dessert comes later. Hopefully it's a treat after another correct answer, but they might get trickier now that we're near the end."

"The Keeper of this one of a kind Red Book must have the exact right memories of the exact right tales so that the True History and True Name of *The Land Between the Seas* is preserved forever."

His french fries gone, the boy started on the second half of his peanut butter and jelly.

"How is your memory, m'boy? Do you remember all the details of the last twelve Red Book tales?

"As you get older you might find that certain experiences are so powerful they cannot be forgotten. The deepest Love. The profoundest Loss. The most thrilling Adventure. The perfect Friendship. Treasure memories, but don't get lost in them. Life is meant to be lived, not remembered."

"This old man stuff is probably a little too early for even a golden young man like you. But one day it might make more sense."

"Brace yourself. Now we confront lucky thirteen, the exact number of original American colonies..."

- 13 - *The Richest Man in All the Land*

***Once Upon a Time, in the Land Between the Seas,* the The Happiest Man in all the Land became The Richest Man the world had ever known.**

No one knows exactly why he was filled with such joy, but most assumed it had something to do with his perfect memory. He even remembered much of what happened before he was born.

Oddly, the Happiest Man claimed that he never thought of the past, nor the future, only the present. That seemed to be the trick. He only used his memory when others asked. Perhaps that's why the Universe decided to hide all the oldest memories with him. He was too in love with the life of now to look much at the mists of

what came before. Knowledge of the past would be safe in a mind like that.

Then this Happiest Man became the Richest Man. It was a disaster for him.

In *The Land Between the Seas*, if you wanted something new you traded for it. That is until wagers between those rooting for the White Wizard and those cheering the Hero Twins created the idea of Money. One thing was chosen as a set value, and then that one thing could be traded back and forth.

The first item used as money were copies of the most famous scroll—*The Journey of William the Dreamer*. Exactly five thousand five hundred and fifty five copies existed.

When that became too limited, the Currency changed and the most valuable object was Secrets. Those with the best Secrets were suddenly rich. But once gossip grew stale, Memories became the new gold. Anyone blessed with deep and wide capacities to remember the past were wealthy beyond measure. The Happiest Man remembered more than anyone and so became the Richest Man

It was tremendous bad luck that the Crookedest Witch in all the Land lived deep in the dark forests surrounding the Happy Man's village.

The Crooked Witch struck immediately. Pretending to be a helpless old woman, she used his kindness to lure him into the woods and captured him. The Witch hid the Happiest and Richest Man in her forest prison that was invisible to anyone except those with dark hearts.

Ransom was what the Crooked Witch desired.

At the very same time, the Twin Heroes on the quest were sitting in the village inn. They were good friends with the Happy

Man and sat thinking about how to save him. Then from the locked third floor window they heard a...

Knock Knock Knock

The Crooked Witch found them. Her knobby knuckles knocked the glass, black boots floating atop of a pair of hovering dark birds of unusual size.

She told the Twins she had a proposition. They had no choice but to listen.

From outside the glass, the mistress of the night asked the Twin Heroes for a sacrifice. In exchange, she would do two things: release the Happy Man and reveal the True Meaning of the Land—the final piece the Twins needed to complete their puzzling adventure.

With a shared nod of understanding, they accepted the price. They knew quests required bravery, walking straight into the dark armed only with hope.

The exchange happened in the center of the town square atop brick of pure yellow, like the corn that grew in all the nearby fields. The Crookedest Witch came perched atop her rotting covered wagon with wheels of charred bone. Stopping in the middle of the growing crowd, she opened the back flap and released the Richest and now once again Happiest Man back to freedom.

In a moment that would become legend, the Hero Twins then made their sacrifice to learn the True Meaning of the Land. They turned to one another, gave the deepest and truest embrace the audience had ever seen, and separated.

Twin A disappeared with the Crooked Witch under the dirty canvas of the wagon. Twin B was left alone in the empty square. He

wished upon the Moon that the separation was only temporary. But he couldn't know for sure.

Quests required bravery. He mustered all he had. Combined with the hope he always carried, the Twin Hero was able to move on, continue the adventure, and pursue his destiny.

Lurking elsewhere in the charming village were whispers that the arrival of the Witch was an omen of an even darker force coming. The entire universe rode atop an invisible tightrope—the Unfathomable Monster might arrive at any moment. Bravery, dear Listener.

- 13 - In the Living Room -

The sun setting, Grandpa now performed the Red Book amid warm floor lamplight. The boy in the blue slippers pulled his fuzzy green blanket under his chin, "Listener on the Quest, we have no time to waste, do you remember coded messages from the past?"

"Here's your riddle:. ***Which Champion would reach the hidden message first?***" Grandpa copied a long code and handed it over...

White Wizard → Turtle Code → 6, Red → 4, Red → 2, Red

Hero Twins → Snake Code → "I Feel great today," Ding →
"What a gorgeous sunrise today," Knock →
"The play today was wonderful," Clap

Did he remember the codes? He searched his mind. One signal meant a message waited, and another meant Urgent. The Snake Code was something about the word "today" and then a sound. The Turtles used numbers and then a color. Was red the correct color to indicate 'Hurry!' What numbers meant a message again? Over 6?

The Storyteller did not give time. "Listener, I need an answer. It is getting far too dark out that window, and the Red Book is telling me the fading is coming."

It felt like the hardest riddle so far, maybe because he was tired. But at least it was one or the other. The boy dug deep into his well of hope, and dreamed his friends were true champions. "The Twin Heroes would win. They sent the correct urgent message. The Turtle numbers and color were wrong."

The boy sat on the edge of the couch, slippers pressed into the carpet. "Wait, wait, wait," Grandpa deciphered a message from the Red Book. "Wait, wait, Maybe, Yes, yes...Correct! Onward m'boy."

The 14th Tale

- 14 - In the Attic -

Absorbed in memories from the box, I hadn't eaten so much as an apple slice since breakfast. Rudy's Pizzeria, the best thin crust this side of the river, was open late. Maybe the best way to honor the Captain was overnight reading with a one quarter cheese, quarter pepperoni, quarter sausage, and quarter supreme.

Exactly seven days after his best pal Wally moved on, Grandpa's blood finished pumping as he slept and Robert Cattrall drifted to his next adventure. I like to think he dreamt and visited *The Land Between the Seas*.

Warm yellow streetlight mixed with a silver blue moonlight drifted across the rafters, and the attic appeared painted by a vintage impressionist. I ordered the pizza, and the call reminded me I needed to cancel the old man's upcoming cardiologist appointment. *Sorry doc, it was his heart that got him in the end.*

I sat in the strapped chair, waited for the thin crust, and tried to guess what was inside the manilla envelope. "Only Open After Finishing the Red Book." Staring at the words, I noticed something I'd missed before. In the bottom corner were the letters CC, in the same sharp vampire script he used during the Red Book reading. Captain Cattrall was a CC after all, born when Calvin Coolidge was President.

That felt like an important clue on the journey, the classic fairy tale adventure for a little boy's golden birthday...

- 14 - In the Living Room -

"Dessert is served for my heroic Listener on the Quest. I'm proud of your calm, intelligence, and bravery." Grandpa yawned as he handed a chocolate sundae to the Boy in the Blue Slippers.

Arms atop the fuzzy green blanket, the boy stifled his own yawn as he spooned the first sweet bite. The darkness out the window, coziness of the couch, and heaviness of the ice cream made him sleepy. But he knew he had to keep his sharpest wits about him in this final stretch of the journey of the Red Book.

Choosing a popsicle for himself, the old man devoured it fast from his chair before it melted into his hand. Between licks he noticed the little one's slightly drooping eyes. "Don't worry, not much longer. Exhaustion sets in near the end of any quest as strenuous as this one."

Grandpa wrapped his popsicle stick in a napkin and set it on the side table. "Before we get to the next story, I want to share an important *Land Between the Seas* mystery. Or rumor. Do you remember the Mysterious Visitor who tried to make everyone's life in the Land a perfect fit for them?"

The boy nodded as he finished his dessert.

"Legend suggests that the Mysterious Visitor is from our very world, yours and mine. Many believe this *Alienus* is the Keeper of the Red Book Secret himself."

Grandpa stared at the boy who scrunched his eyes in eventual understanding. "Wait, You? Were you the Mysterious Visitor?"

"I can't answer any questions until you successfully complete the quest. Remember that all worlds are connected. The Red Book might be one intersection point, like a Gateway.

"I don't understand what that means," the boy said as honestly as possible. "Meanings are tricky."

"Right you are," the old man smiled from his recliner. "Sometimes a meaning is just a feeling."

"Now let's see if your Hero Twins successfully discover the Meaning of the *The Land Between the Seas*. Whatever happens, know that I am very proud of you. Each Listener gets only one chance for this journey, the day before their golden birthday. Most are much older than you when attempting the quest. But you've made it this far at not yet seven. You're a Hero to me, never forget that."

- 14 - *The Creature that Shatters the World of Magic*

Once Upon a Time, in the Land Between the Seas, **the Unfathomable Monster returned and changed the Universe forever.**

It was entirely the fault of the Listener on the Quest and the Reader of this Red Book. Yes, you on page 98.

The collision that led to the Monster might have been inevitable, written in the stars, the product of destiny, or a fluke.

After deep consultation with antique charts and old tomes that crumbled in his hands, the White Wizard believed he finally discovered the True Shape of the Land. He felt his quest complete.

The Wizard rode hard across the Golden Beach that lined the Timeless Lake. He headed toward the castle of the King to spread the good news of his success.

At the very same moment, Twin B was riding on the same Golden Beach in the opposite direction. More alone than ever, the solo Hero felt cut in half without his companion, but clung to the remaining hope burrowed deep inside.

In what some would call a coincidence and some call fate, the White Wizard and Twin B, both lost in daydreams, ran directly into one another. Each nearly collapsed but were able to keep their hands on the reins. A large crowd soon grew, amazed that both Heroes on the quest were together on the same beach.

****PssshhhhAHhhhhhhhHHHBurBurbhbPssss****

Without warning, a bubbling, gurgling, piercing sound unlike any ever heard in the Land broke across the sand in a shockwave. It tossed most to the ground and shattered the trunks of trees hundreds of gallops away.

The Unfathomable Monster rose from the Endless Lake in an ominous spectacle. It appeared as a mountain emerging from the center of the water. Words did not exist in the Land to properly describe the creature and so the crowd found itself inventing new nonsense words that sounded like how the Creature made them feel.

Forms slithered atop the mammoth curved shell of the Mountain. These flexible tendrils of the Monster could take all shapes, turning the top of the beast into trees, grasses, and flowers. Part of the shell was a mound, exactly like the one that spoke with the Green Sage in the ancient tale.

A head emerged that was two heads, long necks, four eyes, an unknown numbers of limbs. The Creature was described differently by all who saw it, depending on where they were standing on the beach. The Monster rose and shifted until the waves finally stopped crashing and the Mountain settled into a new position in the middle of the water, like a large Island drawn up from the bottom of the depths.

It spoke and all listened, "We are One made from Two. Once an Astonishing Snake and Beautiful Turtle, we are now United, and something more more. As they would say in the world of the Red Book, *E Pluribus Unum*."

"You know us as the Protectors of the Magic, the last left who remember the True Name of this place. But our time here grows short, our journey moves to different dimensions. To save this *Land Between the Seas*, new Heroes must bear the burden of the

Memory. Do they exist? Is there anyone here who remembers? Now is the time to speak."

The White Wizard stepped forward and answered the call of the Protectors.

"The True Name of this world," he said without fear, "must be the Original Name. Where it all began."

With his long staff, the wise man walked around and drew a large shape in the sand.

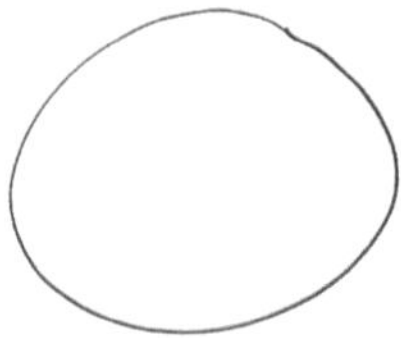

"This is the True Shape of the Land. The Zero or a Circle or a Letter known as 'Oh.' The intersection of Letters, Numbers, Shapes, and Sounds"

The Wizard stood without saying more. The crowd stopped murmuring. Even the wind paused and listened.

"The True Sound of the Land is Silence. Because that is what Nothing sounds like."

"Finally, the True Meaning is Nothing. That is what it represents, because everything starts from Nothing, including all the Land you see."

A murmur rose at the Wizard's genius. The Original Protectors, the Mountain in the Lake, scanned the beach asking, "Anyone else?"

The Twin grew nauseous and unbalanced. He always pictured this moment with his partner. Unlike the Wizard, he had no speech prepared. But he was a Hero on a quest and bravery was

required. Twin B dismounted and went in front of the heads of the Monster.

With a heel, he drew the shape of the Land as they had seen from atop the eagles as large as apple trees. He then whispered the True Sound to the heads of the Protectors, the name of that shape as known in the world of the Red Book.

Twin B paused, unsure what to do next. He had no other answers. If his Best Friend was with him, he and A might be able to use their combined wisdom to find the True Meaning. But by himself on the beach, he felt only a nothingness. Until...

Two shadowy shapes emerged from the crowd—The Crooked Witch and Twin A, his blond hair gently blowing, a large smile on his handsome face.

The Heroes embraced most deep, each feeling whole for the first time since separated.

At that very moment, the Original Protectors, the Unfathomable Monster, boomed a decision, "Correct! The Heroic Twins have demonstrated the Shape, Sound, and Meaning of the True Name of the *The Land Between the Seas.*"

A hush descended on the sand as the words spread from the front of the crowd to the back. Then a boiling cheer rose, rattled, and spiked, causing waves to ripple across the water.

They were saved!

The Protectors continued, "But they couldn't have gotten there alone. The White Wizard's knowledge is essential. To arrive at the True Name you must start with Nothing. Never forget, real magic and meaning comes when two that may appear mirror opposites are able to connect. Everyone is stronger when United."

From the front of the crowd, the Crooked Witch listened with a strange smile. She wasn't crooked at all, only misunderstood, like the Astonishing Snake and Beautiful Turtle. The Witch knew the

only way to share the True Meaning of the Land was not to tell the Heroes, but to make them Feel it.

In the eons to come, legend spread that the Original Protectors, Hero Twins, and White Wizard disappeared together through a hidden cave, to the Bluest Star in the Sky, and into the Universe of the Red Book.

Before leaving the beach on the day of the Unfathomable Monster's return, everyone assembled together, looked up to the purple heavens, and sang a riddle to that Bluest Star...

Now we turn to the blue light in the air,
The key lives inside, the quest ends there.
The answer is three letters, that's what we see.
But to him it's two shapes, they're called M and E.
The key's name is one sound, the same as the last letter
He's hearing this now, or reading it would be better.

The twinkling dots in the lavender sky surged a sudden brightness, as if acknowledging a coded message received. A call down from the heavens. A connection from one world to another.

- 14 - In the Living Room -

"They did it!" the boy bounced on the carpet with arms raised. "I knew they would!"

"They sure did. True Friendship is pure gold."

Grandpa sat down and took a more somber tone, "They did it, but I'm afraid your quest is not yet finished. There are 15 Red Book Tales, remember. And you've only done 14."

"The 15th Tale is hidden behind an exit Gateway. The path unlocks if you answer this Red Book riddle: ***Who is the key in the song sung to the sky?***"

"You have little time to deliberate. The Moon grows bright. Breathe, think, and remember your lessons," the Storyteller encouraged his young ward.

For the first time The Boy in the Blue Slippers knew the answer as if it was planted there by an invisible friend. He solved it as soon as he heard his Grandpa read the riddle from the book.

"The key is ME, two shapes called M and E. But they would say "You." The sound of the key is the same as the sound of the last letter, U." Said the very wise Listener, "They were singing to me."

"Einstein! You've answered a most challenging question. Exactly, little one. You are the key through the Gateway. We've reached the finale."

The 15th Tale

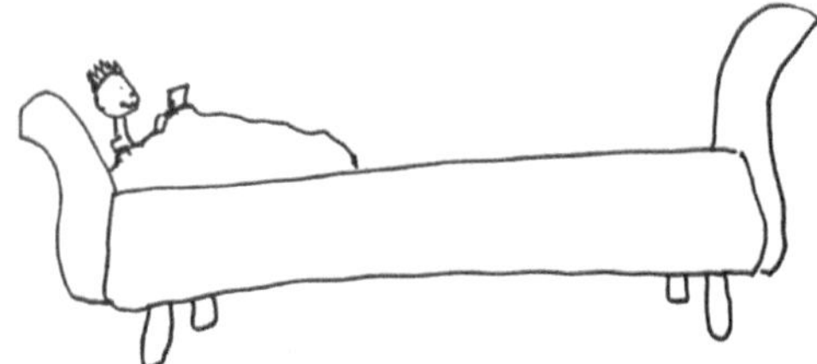

- 15 - In the Attic -

The time had come. A pizza box balanced on a pile of old magazines, the manilla envelope in the box, the Red Book on my lap. I was ready to finally get the answers that I longed for all those years ago.

I noticed my fingers twirling the Blue Star Quarter from the box. I no longer worried about ruining a favorite memory with Grandpa by re-reading the Red Book. *Treasure memories, but don't get lost in them. Life is meant to be lived, not remembered.*

I put the Blue Star Quarter in my pocket. Might be good luck.

With a burst of 7 year old spirit, I peaked at the gold edged pages, full of mystery. Then I opened the Red Book, ready to read out loud to Grandpa's attic, imaging him on a cozy cloud couch, in comfortable slippers, under a fuzzy blue blanket, roles reversed, the old man once again becoming the young Listener on the Quest...

- 15 - In the Living Room -

Grandpa ran a hand through his hair, then pressed two fingers under his chin, "I'm afraid you are close but still far away."

The boy knew what must come next. "I must figure out the True Name. The Shape, Sound, and Meaning that the Hero Twins discovered. That's why it was kept secret in the tale. It's my final test, isn't it?"

"You are wise beyond your almost golden years. That is exactly correct," the current Keeper of the Red Book looked like a coach before sending his team out for the final play of the Super Bowl. "I have endless faith in you, m'boy."

"Remember the history of *The Land Between the Seas*. It's a story of connections, between those who are the same, and those who are different. Everything you need is given to you. I can't answer any questions, but the rules do let me share secret coded clues that might help. There are multiple paths to victory. It doesn't matter how you get there, only that you fulfill your destiny."

Grandpa then rattled off three sets of bizarre clues. It felt like they could only be understood by those who knew an invisible language, hidden messages between two best friends, like the Hero Twins, who can read one another's minds.

"Remember the history of the Land
Start with Nothing.
Then it becomes Something with a Name."
Then the Land Splits.
In Two Like a Mirror.

Each Side Changes, Sharpens.
Connects Again.
Becomes the True Shape.
E Pluribus Unum."

Three seconds of silence in the living room, then Grandpa shared the second clue...

"Sometimes a Word is a single Letter.
Vampire Letters
When Combined
They make a New Shape Altogether."

Then the final, strange hidden message...

"A Shape can have a Name.
A Name is a series of Letters.
Letters are squiggles that have a Sound.
A Sound Means Something.
The Meaning is often a Feeling."

The Storyteller did not explain further. Moonbeams filtered through the living room, shining a spotlight on the showman as he finished his performance, " This last challenge must be taken alone. I will be working in the other room while you complete the quest. Eventually I'll return and we'll discover if the deepest fading begins or if you've saved the world of magic and wonder forever."

The Keeper of the Red Book Secret left the Boy in the Blue Slippers alone to his thoughts. The sound of a shutting door echoed through the hall, into the living room, and under the fuzzy green blanket on the couch. It came down to this. With all the hope he could muster, the almost golden boy tapped his 'ol box in the attic, and jumped headfirst into the Red Book...

- 15 - *The Boy in the Blue Slippers Who Tried to Save Magic*

Once Upon a Time, in the Land Between the Seas, **the Listener on the Quest, the Boy in the Blue Slippers, embarked on his final Red Book Mission in hopes of saving US All.**

Every creature in the Land watched the Mysterious Listener from another world with hope, wonder, worry, and amazement. The King and The Marys stared at the skies together from the castle tower. The Crooked Witch, now known as the Wise Witch, cheered the Boy with her new friends. Everyone rooted for the Hero from Another Dimension.

The Boy in the Blue Slippers wisely positioned himself inside a castle made almost entirely of impenetrable brick. Wolves, thieves, and hobgoblins stood no chance of penetration. It might even have withstood a dragon blast. He could ponder the riddle in complete safety.

He wore garments of the most comfortable material and was kept warm by his green cape. The boy had shoes that provided perfect flexibility and were of the exact shade of blue as the magical star in our sky. They fit only the wisest of sages.

Before departing for unknown lands, the Boy's mentor and guide on the quest gifted him several magical objects to help on the arduous mental journey.

These included a blank notebook with all white pages. The mentor knew that the best ideas start from nothing. He also provided a small green stick that made permanent marks on any surface. The Boy was gifted knives positioned together, known as skizzorz, a string tied in a circle with unknown powers, and a brand new Eagle Quarter—a magical currency of greatest luck.

The fate of the entire Land depended on this Hero from another world, the Boy in the Blue Slippers, correctly identifying the Shape, Sound, and Meaning of the True Name. Can he save us?

Alone but safe in his castle, armed with his tools, the Boy dove into the Red Book Riddle.

Unsure where to begin, the young Listener remembered how the Heroes in the tales started their journeys. The White Wizard figured out the Meaning first, and then the Sound, and finally the Shape. But where would the Boy find a meaning from nothing?

Instead he decided to follow the path of the two friends, the Hero Twins. If he could figure out the True Shape of the Land, then the other pieces might fall into place. He imagined riding eagles high in the clouds like the Heroes. Maybe in his dreams.

The Boy in the Blue Slippers thought on the coded clues left to him by his mentor and guide on the quest.

Luckily the young Hero had an uncanny memory. *Start with Nothing... Get a Name... Break in Two... Change... Come back together*

The Boy scribbled on the paper, trying to understand shapes. He knew the Wizard started with Nothing. He drew a large Zero on the notebook with the greenmark stick. He stared at the flat shape.

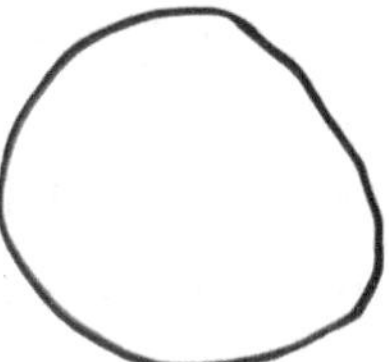

Then he lifted the string and made the same shape in the air, a circle or a zero. The intersection of letters and numbers. He remembered that the Land started from this Shape, the Nothing. But it became something else. It's True Shape. What could that be? *What Shape did Twin B draw in the sand with his heel?* If the Boy knew that, he'd be able to figure out the rest.

He considered a Triangle, because it had three sides. Three was a magical number in the Land, like in all fairy tales. There were three parts to the True Name.

But he couldn't make the Triangle fit the other clues. What would be the Meaning of a Triangle?

The Boy grabbed the string and wiggled it around into whatever came to mind. Maybe it was a complicated shape, so he began thinking outside the box. He formed the circle into a brain. Then he tried to transform the string into the shape of his country, the United States of America. Neither felt right.

Suddenly the Hero felt a sting on his chest. Looking down he saw the twin knives known as skizzorz poking through his garments into his skin. *Eureka*!

His mentor gave these for a reason. The Land *breaks in two*. The Boy took the tool and snipped the tied string circle at the top and bottom, creating two smaller strings, each half the size.

The Boy felt he was on the right path, but he didn't yet know the next step. The Land split in two, *like mirror opposites facing each other*. Both strings might mirror each other. But what shape? Then he heard the second coded clue—*Sometimes a single letter is a word... Vampire letters... Combined... Make a new shape.*

He remembered the answer to the last Gateway riddle, YOU. The third letter sounded the exact same as the entire word. You and U. *Sometimes a word is a letter.* He was getting warmer. If two vampire letters combine they make the True Shape of *The Land Between the Seas*. But what other letter sounds like an entire word?

Stumped, he wished his mentor had left him the lucky Blue Star Quarter, instead of a blank new one.

All magic comes from Nothing. Inspired, he used his marking stick and drew a green star atop his eagle. *I'm a magician too*, he remembered, and could make his own lucky quarter.

Almost immediately, it came to him.

If he was the key, then his letters would matter. *What were important letters to ME*? He pondered from the soft clouded cushions behind his impenetrable brick walls. The Boy in the Blue Slippers thought of himself as a Gemini, a magically combined creation, when two become one and then into something much more.

Eureka!

The Land Between the Seas. Seas. Letters are Sounds. Seas. Two Cs. His mentor was know as CC. Important letters for the family.

The boy used the strings to shape the two mirrored Cs, as if an O was cut in half, then drifted apart. But the boy did not stop there. *Each Side Changes, Sharpens. Vampire letters.*

The young Hero knew what that meant. Letters don't always look the same, but it only matters that the meaning remains. The Boy shaped the Cs with sharp points, the way his mentor drew them.

Combining them, he revealed the True Shape of the Land. The same one drawn in the sand by Hero Twin B.

***Eureka*!**

The shape was known in the Universe of the Red Book. The Hero now need only to connect the Shape with a Sound and Meaning.

Like all pairs of Legends, it was as if he and his guide shared a mind. His mentor's final clue echoed in his attic box. *Shapes have Names...Letters are Squiggles that Make a Sound...The Meaning is often a Feeling."*

The Twin Heroes won without saying a word. They hugged one another. They felt something True.

That's all he needed. The Boy opened a fresh white page. In his lucky green, he drew the True Shape of the Land. Underneath in

squiggly letters, he wrote the True Name of the Shape. He finished with more letters representing the Meaning of it all.

Not one to settle for average, the Key from the Universe of the Red Book knew he would answer the final riddle in 3 dimensions, not the 2D of the white notebook. When his mentor returned, he would show the True Shape with the string, then make the True Sound of the shape out loud for the ear, finishing with a large bear hug so he could feel the True Meaning. *The Meaning is often a Feeling.*

Even in the darkest emptiness, blind and deaf, with nothing to see or hear, you can always Remember to Feel.

Using the strength, speed, and wisdom of the greatest Heroes, the Boy in the Blue Slippers, Listener on the Quest, and potential Keeper of the Red Book completed his long journey. He snuggled under his warm green cape, his magical slippers keeping his feet warm, and he waited for his companion on the journey.

The Boy drifted into dreamland, and for the first time arrived in a place he'd only heard about in stories—*The Land Between the Cs.* They rushed him to a castle and claimed him the Victorious Hero who Saved the World...

CHAPTER 16

- 16 - In the Attic -

All those years ago, I found my solution to the Quest, and fell straight asleep. An exhausted golden 7 year old's marathon finished.

When I woke up the next morning, Grandpa was gone. He'd been called to an emergency, the other side of the planet needed his talents. Robert Cattrall was an important man.

I never discovered if I succeeded in the quest. Every time I asked, he did not have the book with him. He'd say things like, "you'll learn at the right time."

I've waited decades to discover if my answer to the Red Book riddle was the correct one. Now this 'ol box in the attic finally gave me what I wanted. The Red Book was mine.

I peaked under the cover for the first time ever. In blue marker, I saw his handwritten answer to the 15th and Final Riddle.

In my head, the attic echoed with what he'd say, "Correct! My Golden Grandson, the Genius. The rarest of rare, Triple Gs. The new Keeper of the Red Book Secret!"

I sat and savored my victory—The Shape and Sound of The Heart. The Meaning is Love. But Love is not really a shape, or string, or letters, or a word, or a sound. The magical storyteller taught that it must be the most important Feeling in all the Universe.

Something as simple as a hug from the exact person at the exact right time with the exact right meaning blooms into the most beautiful Feeling you ever experience.

I turned to the second page of the Red Book, Blank. Then the next, Blank. Blank. The Red Book was all white nothing.

My laugh echoed rafters and trusses. Grandpa loved the long joke. *The Land Between the Seas* came directly from his 'ol box in the attic. The most special thing he had, better than the fastest supercomputer in the world.

Setting the Red Book in the box, I grabbed the Blue Star Quarter and examined it in a palm. With a smile I reached into my own pocket and pulled out a second quarter. It also had a handwritten star on the back, this one in green. I'd carried it with me for luck since the day before my golden birthday, all those years ago. I held Grandpa's Blue Star and my Green Star Quarter in the same hand. The two lucky charms finally United.

I picked up the old string, tied, cut, then re-tied. I made a circle. As an adult, I noticed that it could be turned into a heart without splitting in two. You need only tug at the top and pull toward the center, and a heart emerges.

But perhaps that misses the point.

Maybe the journey is what matters. The most important lessons, astonishing adventures, and beautiful memories might only be found by those who take the long way. You can never discover the magic of two becoming one without first breaking apart.

I put the manilla envelope on my knees, "Only Open After Finishing the Red Book." I heard Grandpa cheer in the attic, "Onward, m'boy..."

Epilogue

- In the Front Yard -

Honk Honk Honk

Not again!

The grey Audi bleated once more. I silenced the machine and looked for the cats or squirrels who were triggering the alarm. Nothing but the streetlights, vintage yard flamingo, bird bath, and unplugged zen water fountain.

The manilla envelope burned in my hands. I opened it, suddenly ravenous for any final message from Grandpa.

Inside I found a stack of paper, with a handwritten note from the old man on top. My final letter from the world famous letter writer, whose favorite letters were C, P, L, E, and A.

Dear Golden Boy-

I spent a lifetime exploring my 'ol box in the attic. What an adventure it's been. I could pull such magic and wonder from it. It's the birthplace of the Red Book and The Land Between the Seas. As you now know. Straight from up here—Imagine me with three taps above an ear. Ha Ha Ha!

Then I remembered (pesky memories), that the 'ol box in the attic is the one thing that YOU can never fully know. Because it's all mine, like yours is all yours. That's why I included this story on white printed paper. It is my first and last attempt to pull something out of this aging cardboard box and leave it for you to explore.

We have the Red Book, I like to think of my tale as the White Book. If I live long enough, I'll write a Blue Book. Red, White, then Blue. It's poetic, don't you think? If I don't make it, you'll have to finish it for me.

Versions of this story have bounced around my head for eons, starting in life's mistiest times. Now it arrives in this box to you in the form of letters, words, and paragraphs. I share it in the hope that you can find some of its many hidden meanings. Meanings are usually Feelings. Never forget to Feel.

Love Always to You, My First, Maybe Only, Favorite Reader,
Grandpa

I flipped to the next page to discover a typed story with an underlined title, **The Hero with No Name**. Was this his best recollection of his Red Book tale, made up in his head all those years ago?

I didn't read more, because a minivan pulled up. It was Lucy, a friend who helped Grandpa in his later years. She'd come to check the mail before heading to her night shift.

Noticing the papers in my hand, she said, "Oh I didn't know he wrote it down."

"You know about this?" I asked. Jealous for a moment that he told anyone else except me that he wrote a story.

"No no. He would never tell me," Lucy admitted, "But I overheard him reading parts out loud in his office. Or maybe it was to Mr. Powers on the phone. It might be about his time in the War, but I couldn't know."

"War?"

"He and Mr. Powers talked all about it. General Maymerry. D Day. Omaha Beach. Quite the experience for a young man, I suspect. But he sure had a life afterwards. What an astonishing man." Lucy gave a sympathetic smile and drove off.

My birthday is June 7th. He created the Red Book tales, *The Land Between the Seas,* and shared it with me on June 6th. D-Day.

The Moon followed me as I went back into Grandpa's house, grabbed a midnight pizza snack, and settled on the couch, under a cozy blue blanket, I became the master storyteller's very first reader...

The Hero With No Name

By

Captain Robert "CC" Cattrall

"Once Upon A Time, a young man awoke face down in a bed of sand, with no memory of where he was or how he arrived. His husk brown boots pointed to endless waters behind him, crashing in a rough surf. He wore green garments stretched across a fit frame, and a face of confused intense curiosity. He wasn't scared..."

Paul Alan Richardson

Paul drifts here and there, usually west of the Blue Ridge Mountains. He enjoys nature's curious creatures, games, mystery, and beautiful cosmic nonsense. He lives in the Shenandoah Valley of Northern Virginia, surrounded by family, friends, two springer spaniels, and a mysterious calico cat.

Paul's first book is *Welcome to Willouby: An American Fairy Tale* (The Blue Book).

www.paulalanrichardson.com

Book Club Conversations

1. Knowing the differences between the two groups after reading this tale, are your more a Turtle, Snake, or mix of both?

2. Grandpa draws a Woodsman and mentions the Tin Man, because he was searching for a Heart. At his funeral his friend said he had a heart three sizes too big. The book is filled with clues about the solution to the True Name question. Did you catch any other hints?

3. The secret is ultimately about letters, specifically the combination of one letter – C. How many clues and references can you find in the text hinting at the importance of the Letter C?

4. Friendship, in all its forms, plays a key role in this tale. The Hero Twins embrace near the end was the real example of the true Meaning of the heart, Love. Do you agree that a true friend is one who loves you without any desire to change who you are?

5. *The Land Between the Seas* is created when Nothing twists into Something and becomes Everything. It then gives itself a Name. Does the idea of Something coming from Nothing fit your thoughts about the real world? Is this any different than our universe starting from some unknown place, a Big Bang or a Creator?

6. The man in the attic delays opening the Red Book out of fear that he'd ruin a favorite memory. Have you ever not done something in order to keep a treasured memory alive? Do you think a memory can be ruined or tarnished?

7. Grandpa said that he thought he could reach this magical Land in his dreams. Have any dreams stuck with you and felt like they might be some message or have important meaning?

8. The Mysterious Visitor (who might be Grandpa) granted one wish to the Land. He interpreted their wish as making the *The Land Between the Seas* something like our idea of Heaven, where everyone's life was exactly what they wanted. Do you think they picked the right method to decide Heaven, having friends design it? Would you have come up with a different way to determine it? Or picked a different wish altogether?

9. In their dual quests to save the world, the Heroes chose different paths. The White Wizard used intellect, research, and careful deduction to solve the riddle. The Twins relied more on fate and destiny in hopes that the Universe would guide them to the answer. If you were on the quest, which approach would you take?

www.ingramcontent.com/pod-product-compliance
Lightning Source LLC
Chambersburg PA
CBHW060801310726
48980CB00002B/191

* 9 7 9 8 9 9 9 9 5 5 0 0 5 *